THE CURSE OF BLOODSTONE

Borgo Press Books by VICTOR J. BANIS

THE CURSE OF BLOODSTONE

A GOTHIC
NOVEL OF TERROR

V. J. BANIS

THE BORGO PRESS

MMXII

THE CURSE OF BLOODSTONE

FIRST BORGO PRESS EDITION

Published by Wildside Press LLC

www.wildsidebooks.com

DEDICATION

I am deeply indebted to my friend, Heather, for all the help she has given me in getting these early works of mine reissued.

And I am grateful as well to Rob Reginald, for all his assistance and support.

CONTENTS

CHAPTER ONE

The black ship with its blood-red sails moved slowly toward the distant horizon, casting a shadow under the moon while the storm raged and howled.

A young woman stood high on the cliff watching the ship as it grew smaller and smaller. She leaned into the wind, peering through her tears to catch a last and final glimpse of the ship—and found herself falling, falling, falling....

* * * * * *

Vanessa thrashed and twisted deeper into the tangle of bedclothes. Still clutched in the grip of the dream, she could feel the coldness of the sea, yet its biting wetness did not penetrate her night clothes.

She knew it was a dream, yet she did not want to awaken from it. She had found him again, and again he had abandoned her.

She wanted to stay in that thunder-black mist; to stand forever atop that high cliff, but the dream was ended; it always ended there with her falling into the turbulent waters.

Vanessa stirred, but refused to open her eyes. She knew the welcome darkness would be gone and it would be daylight. The sea would be calm and clear, rolling silently under the bright blue of a sky unbroken by clouds. The black, plunging rocks of the dream would turn tan and pink and shimmer with trickles of water as they lazed at the ocean's edge, the world changing from black to bright.

Through her tears she saw him standing in the bow, waving his farewell. The bloodstone flashed and gleamed as his hand moved; its beam hypnotized her, as it always did. She felt herself being drawn into its depths, its ruby-black abyss. He was no more now than a shadow on the deck, but the ring continued to spark and glint.

The tears burned on her cheeks. She knew her tears would never bring him back to her. But there would be other dreams. She only lived for and in those dreams.

"Bloodstone." She said it aloud. Yes, that was it, that was where the answer must lie. She would go home to Bloodstone, where the dreams had started, long ago.

She put her arms over her head and stretched. The dream lingered, but merely as a happy memory now. She felt she had spent all of her twenty-three years searching and finding the things that made her happy, only to have them vanish. She had fled Bloodstone and her loving parents. Tutrice, her old Cajun guardian told her she was afraid of real happiness; Vanessa had scoffed and said she would know real happiness when she saw it.

And she *had* encountered it. But each and every time it centered on him—the man with the bloodstone on his finger. And she always lost him.

"You dreamed," Tutrice said as she came into the bedroom carrying a breakfast tray of inlaid ivory and tortoise. The delicate, rose-patterned china tinkled softly in the brightness of the morning.

Vanessa felt a tinge of disappointment at not being able to surprise her old guardian with the news that she'd had the same wonderful dream again. But Tutrice always knew everything. Tutrice was older than life itself, and being so old, knew all things even before anyone else knew them.

"Birds will nest in that furrowed brow," Tutrice said as she reached out and smoothed back the frown lines. "That dream is not good, my child. It makes you unhappy."

Vanessa picked up a piece of buttered toast and bit daintily into its edge. She tasted nothing, only the bitterness that came with the end of her dream. She wished Tutrice would go away. Her presence was unnerving. Yet Vanessa knew she could not think of living without Tutrice hovering over her, protecting her, doting on her every want and need.

"I like my dreams," Vanessa said, more out of defiance than anything else.

"Ah, what is there to like about those nightmares? They always end so badly." Tutrice stood beside the bed, leaning slightly against one of the massive fluted bed posts. "You waste your time with things that can never be."

Vanessa tossed the uneaten piece of bread back onto its plate. She glowered at the old woman. "It can be," she said. "It must be."

Tutrice let out a sigh. "It will never be. You know it will never be."

"I know no such thing," Vanessa said angrily. "Go away, you old crone. Leave me to eat and think."

Tutrice laughed. "You fancy yourself like the rest," she said. "Remember this, my little one. You are not like the rest. You are not. Listen to what I tell you and do not deceive yourself. You lost your chance at happiness; you will never find it again."

"I will." Vanessa tossed her serviette across the tray and shoved it roughly aside, spilling the contents of the coffee cup.

Tutrice shook her head. She said nothing, merely took up the tray and started out of the room.

Vanessa glared at her as she moved away. "Wait," she said. "I want our trunks packed immediately. I am going back to Bloodstone."

Tutrice stood quite still with her back turned. Then her shoulders squared themselves. Slowly she turned and leveled her eyes on the young girl in the bed. "That may not be wise, child," Tutrice said glumly.

"Wise or not, we are going."

"A storm is brewing."

"I don't care about your storms. Don't try to dissuade me, Tutrice." She glanced toward the windows. "I see no signs of a storm."

"Nevertheless," the old woman said, "a hurricane is in the wind."

"What is that to me?" Vanessa asked as she swung her legs over the side of the bed and stood, letting her filmy nightdress cascade down around her feet. She lifted her long, dark hair from the back of her neck and let her finger trail through the tresses, and went toward the casement windows. "There isn't a single cloud in the sky."

"Just because you do not see things does not mean they are not there."

Vanessa spun around, her eyes flashing. "Do you always get pleasure from thwarting my plans? We are going to Bloodstone. Pack, I say, immediately."

"Oh, child, why do you persist in torturing yourself? Bloodstone is in the past. You cannot find what you seek in that wretched place."

"Wretched? Bloodstone is my home...it is your home too, remember that."

"No one place is my home," the old Cajun woman said, her eyes darkening, her mouth disappearing into the mass of wrinkles. "My home is nowhere, as is yours, child. Forget Bloodstone."

"Never. We came from Bloodstone. We will return to it."

The breakfast dishes rattled on the tray. "Very well, child. We will go. But remember, I warned you against it. You will not find what you seek at Bloodstone." She went out, her back ramrod straight.

The old woman was incorrigible, Vanessa told herself. Yet she knew she would be completely lost without Tutrice. Vanessa had never known a moment when the old woman was not there to guard and protect her.

It was all well and good, however, to have a devoted guardian, but Tutrice was becoming more and more her keeper. And of late, Tutrice was becoming more and more domineering. Ever since the accident.

No, she could not think of that accident. She'd lost him and if it weren't for Tutrice she too would be lying dead at the bottom of the sea. But at least she would have been with him, Tutrice had saved her from that watery grave but she hadn't wanted to be saved. She would have gone willingly to her death, just so long as he was beside her.

Thunder boomed. Vanessa glanced up, astonished at the sound of thunder on such a glorious day. It was as if the thunder roll was in answer to her thoughts. A shiver coursed through her. She wrapped her arms around her and stepped away from the windows. She couldn't be certain, but she thought the day was suddenly darkening. It seemed an impossibility. Surely it was merely her mood and her imagination.

Again the sound of distant, ominous thunder echoed over the sea, like a warning.

CHAPTER TWO

Savage ocean waves crashed and pounded against the high sea cliff, gnawing away at its foundation. The angry, howling wind whipped up over the bluff and across the housetops. It toppled chimneys, ripped shutters from houses, doors from hinges, uprooted trees and fences as it cut a path across the village of Skull Point. The people of Skull Point had not seen the likes of such a storm since the night Vanessa Mallory went away, five years before.

And now, Vanessa Mallory was back, or at least Simon Caldwell said so. When Simon told them the news, they stared in disbelief. Such news was almost as frightening as the hurricane that threatened to tear them from their homes. Simon Caldwell must be mistaken, they thought. It just couldn't be so. Vanessa Mallory could not have returned to Skull Point. Vanessa Mallory was dead.

"I saw her," Simon Caldwell insisted. "I saw her with my own two eyes, I tell you. I watched her landau barrel over the stone bridge at the end of Noah Bingham's property, streak down Willow Lane, and race straight through the center of town—toward Bloodstone."

The small, select group of townspeople who were clustered around the great open fire in Simon Caldwell's kitchen just continued to stare at him. Simon saw the disbelief in their eyes. "You wouldn't be thinking me to be a liar?" he challenged.

Jenny Hastings gave Martha Wilkins a questioning glance; Martha shook her head, cautioning Jenny to keep her thoughts to herself. Jenny gave a resigned sigh and nodded. They knew better than to disagree with Simon Caldwell. This was Simon's house, their refuge from the storm; the newest and strongest brick-and-mortar building in all of Skull Point; their only stronghold against the fury of the hurricane that raged outside.

Simon Caldwell, their appointed mayor, didn't offer the safety of his house without reason, and more than mere loyalty would be expected of them once the storm was spent. Simon would expect repayment—not always direct monetary payment, of course, but payment of a type that would make them forever dependent upon Simon Caldwell for the livelihood of the town as well as for themselves.

There was Noah Bingham's house, of course. But Noah Bingham was merely a fisherman and not quite on their social level. Besides, Noah lived at the other end of town and took no interest in their social and political affairs.

Of course there was the Mallory mansion—Bloodstone. They might seek shelter there. After all, Bloodstone was a larger and stronger refuge than either Noah Bingham's or Simon Caldwell's. The old stone mansion on the bluff had withstood more violent storms than anyone could remember. But no one went to Bloodstone. Death lived within its walls.

"I tell you, I saw her," Simon Caldwell said in the face of their doubtful expressions. "She had that old Cajun woman with her, Tutrice."

* * * * * *

Noah Bingham had seen Vanessa also.

Noah's house, like Simon Caldwell's, was crowded with neighbors huddled together to ride out the storm. They weren't of the social ilk that Simon Caldwell attracted. They were farmers and fishermen who lived on the periphery of Skull Point—the hard-working people who never bothered much with the affairs of their so-called "city cousins" who lived in the town proper.

No one argued with Noah's announcement. If Noah had

seen Vanessa Mallory, then Vanessa Mallory must indeed have returned to Skull Point...to Bloodstone.

"Then she isn't dead," Zeb Brewster said.

"Appears not, Zeb. I saw her real clear, and that old Indian woman was with her." Noah shook his head slowly. "I can't tell you where she come from, but she's back all right."

"But she was drowned," Brewster's wife said. "Five years back."

Noah shrugged. "That's what they said, Caroline. But I saw what I saw. Vanessa Mallory rode over my bridge no more than a few hours ago."

The wind suddenly started to pound more violently against the outside of the house. They heard a shutter being ripped from its hinges. A window shattered somewhere in one of the upstairs rooms.

Noah's wife gasped and quickly got to her feet.

"No, Ruth. You'd best stay put. No tellin' what's going on in the rest of the house. We're safest here in the kitchen."

Ruth gave her husband an anxious look. "I'll just go into the next room and make sure the children are all right."

Noah nodded. The overhead beams creaked and groaned. "She left in a storm just like this one," Noah said. "It was this time of year too...almost to the day."

* * * * * * *

In Simon Caldwell's kitchen the elite of the town did not worry about their heavily boarded windows. There was no reason to worry; everything was safe and secure. The howling of the storm didn't seem to interfere with the whispers that buzzed among them. Even their own individual houses seemed to be of no importance. What was damaged, Simon would see was repaired. What was irreparable, Simon would see was replaced. The land would remain, and that was all that was of significance. The land was theirs and no one, not even the heavens themselves, was able to take that away from them,

But the return of Vanessa Mallory brought fear into their souls. The land once belonged to the Mallorys. Vanessa might make claim to all these properties now that she wasn't dead and had returned to Skull Point.

Martha Wilkins expressed her fears openly.

"How can she make claim for the land?" Jenny Hastings asked her. "Her parents deeded it over to the town."

"That's right," her husband agreed. Sam Hastings never disagreed with anyone, especially his wife. "Even if she isn't dead, Vanessa can't take what is rightfully the town's own property."

Simon Caldwell shook his head. "Vanessa's back to make trouble though," he predicted. "The Mallorys always make trouble." He sucked air through the gap in his front teeth. "But everyone here has a stake in Skull Point and we've been doing pretty good since we took over the Mallory properties. Noah Bingham and his crowd don't give a hang about what happens here; all they care about is their precious little boats and farms. It's up to us to stand up to Vanessa if she intends to make trouble for us."

Everybody was quick to agree, all nodding their heads and mumbling their support for whatever Simon intended to do. The town had prospered since the Mallorys relinquished the land to them. None of them wanted to lose any of the advantages they had gained from such transfer of title.

* * * * * * *

Noah Brewster wasn't worried about Vanessa making trouble. He reached for his pipe and stuck it between his teeth. His bright, handsome eyes danced as the flame of the match touched the tobacco bowl. He sucked in his fat cheeks as he puffed the pipe to life. "Old Simon must be fit to be tied," he chuckled.

"Do you think he knows Vanessa is back?" his wife asked as she closed the door that connected the children's room and the kitchen.

Noah chuckled again. "Simon knows all right," he said. "Old Simon don't miss a trick." He sat back down on the stool and put an elbow to a knee and leaned toward the fire.

Zeb Brewster suddenly got to his feet and started pacing. "It's all well and good for you to think lightly of all this, Noah," Zeb said. "You ain't got no interest in the land. You're a fisherman. Your boats and tack is all you care about. But what about me and Jonah here? We work our lands and we've been doing pretty good since old Simon's been running things."

Jonah Black and his wife, Rachel, sat at the large, square kitchen table that had been pulled up close to the hearth. "Yes," Jonah agreed. "Zeb's and my property are two of the biggest farms in these parts. Since title changed hands, we find ourselves a lot better off."

"Simon don't give us any trouble at all," Rachel put in.

"Not yet, he won't," Noah said as he continued to puff leisurely on his pipe. "You just wait, Rachel. Old Simon will tighten the reins on you before long."

"How can he? The property isn't solely his. It belongs to the town...to all of us," Caroline Brewster said.

Noah glanced at her. "Now, Caroline, you know Simon better'n that. Once he and those highfalutin friends of his gets control of something, they'll figure out some way of running the whole shebang. Oh, they'll do it all right and legal and proper like, but in the end they'll wind up owning everything and you'll all be right back where you started."

Zeb jumped to his feet. His wife put a hand on his arm but he shook it off. "I don't agree with you, Noah," he said angrily. "Simon Caldwell and his crowd don't have no claim on my farm now."

"Don't he?" Noah asked sagely, narrowing his eyes to give his question the proper degree of seriousness he meant to convey. "Do you have sole claim to your farm, Zeb?"

Zeb floundered. "Well, no," he stammered. "It ain't mine and Caroline's outright. But it ain't Simon Caldwell's neither."

Noah sucked smoke into his mouth. The howling storm was the only sound in the room. Finally Noah glanced up at Zeb. "Jeremiah Mallory deeded your farm and all the rest of his property over to Skull Point," he said. "Skull Point is run by Simon Caldwell. You and me and everybody else is run by Simon Caldwell."

"But what about the council? We have a town council," Caroline argued. Caroline Brewster was a big woman and her voice matched her size.

"And who, may I ask, is on that town council, Caroline? I'll tell you," Noah answered. "Simon Caldwell, Sam Hastings, Will Wilkins, and four or five other close, intimate chums of old Simon's...all of whom, I might add, are deeply in Simon's personal debt."

Rachel Black leaned across the table. "Well, we're not in Simon's personal debt."

Noah merely smiled. "You're not on the council, neither," he said. He put his pipe back between his teeth and bit into the stem. The whipping, screeching wind and rain lashed against the house. A sudden, appalling crash made everyone stand up. The noise cut through the room like the blade of an ax.

"Glory be," Caroline groaned, making the sign of the cross. Her husband went toward the window. He couldn't possibly have seen out through the heavy wooden shutters. He just stood there staring at the boarded window.

"A tree," he said softly, nervously. "I guess it was just another tree."

From beyond the closed door a child started to cry. The women glanced toward the sleeping room beyond. Ruth started toward it.

"No, Ruth," Rachel Black said. "I'll go see."

Ruth went to stand in front of the fire. She rubbed her hands nervously, bringing circulation back into her chilled fingers. "There won't be no land to worry about if this storm don't let up," she said. Her lips were thin and white, her face pale and drawn. Her nervousness and fright were responsible for her turning sharply on her husband. "It's bad enough for us to be upset about this storm without you upsetting us with other problems."

Caroline Brewster was suddenly as jumpy as the others. "Why do you say 'problem,' Ruth?" she wanted to know. "The deeding of the land to the town was no problem until you and Noah here made it into one."

Noah leaned back and tried to look as calm as possible. "It's Simon Caldwell who will create the problem." He bit hard on the stem of the pipe and wished he'd given a little more forethought to his remark. Everybody was becoming more and more unnerved.

* * * * * * *

The men and women in Simon Caldwell's kitchen were as composed as a group of spectators at a music recital. Simon Caldwell's long, bony face, however, was screwed into a frown. He was thinking about the land, but it wasn't the deed to the lands that troubled him. Vanessa Mallory's presence in Skull Point was his problem. What did she want?

Sam Hastings echoed his question. "I wonder why Vanessa came back here to the Point?"

Simon shrugged. "Where else would she go, Sam? This is her home."

"But she left it to run off after that sea captain, or whatever he was."

His wife gave an admonishing huff. "Wild! That's the only word to describe Vanessa Mallory. Just like her granddaddy. Wild!"

Simon rubbed his bristled chin. "Maybe so, Jenny. But something happened inside Bloodstone these five years ago, something that we don't know about. Jeremiah and Hester would never say what it was, but I know something happened there. Vanessa didn't run off into that storm for no reason."

"There was that sea captain," Martha Wilkins reminded him.

"No, there was something else. I just know there was," he said.

Simon's craggy old face caught the reflection of the fire. To the others he looked exactly like what the children of the town called him: Mr. Skull Point—not because of his position in the town, but because at times like this Simon Caldwell looked more like a bleached skull than anything else. The cheeks were sunken, the eyes deep set and ringed with dark, grayish circles.

Simon was an oddity to look at and to add to his oddity he had no wife—never had one—which made him seem more queer, especially to the children of the town. The older folk—those close to Simon—knew there had been a woman in his life at one time. Simon had loved her more than life itself, but Hester Cartwright had married Jeremiah Mallory and Simon Caldwell had adopted bachelorhood and sworn never to love again.

Simon sighed. "I don't know, Jenny. I just don't know," he said. "But it's something."

"You don't think Vanessa is going to try to get back the deed to the properties, do you, Simon?" Will Wilkins asked.

"How can she?" Simon said. "I'll wave the deeds in front of her pretty nose. What can she do?"

Simon moved a little away from the heat of the fire and studied his friends for a moment. "We don't have a deed to Bloodstone," he said. "The mansion wasn't included in the list of properties."

"I wonder why?" Jenny Hastings asked. "They thought Vanessa dead. Who else would Jeremiah and Hester deed it to but us?"

"Us? You mean 'the town' don't you, Jenny?" Martha Wilkins corrected.

"Same thing," Will said, giving his wife a hard look.

Martha lowered her eyes and fumbled with some imaginary object in her lap.

"Perhaps old Jeremiah deeded it over to some relative we don't know about...maybe one of Hester's people," Sam said.

"There aren't any relatives," Simon told him. "Jeremiah; his wife, Hester; his daughter, Vanessa, that's the lot of them."

"That old house should be torn down before it falls down," Will Wilkins said as he adjusted his more-than-ample frame deeper into the soft chair in which he was sitting.

"Lord, I wouldn't go near that old place for love or money," his wife said.

Jenny Hastings laughed. "Now, don't tell me you believe those tired old stories about its being haunted, Martha. Why, this is 1851." Jenny Hastings was a modern, worldly woman, or so she considered herself.

"The place is haunted," Martha insisted.

"Nonsense. There aren't such things as ghosts any more. They went out in our granddaddy's time."

Simon rubbed the bristles on his chin. "Oh, I wouldn't go so far as to say that, Jenny. Ghosts are ghosts. They've always been and they'll always be."

Simon Caldwell, however, wasn't thinking about ghosts. He was thinking about Bloodstone. He was thinking about Vanessa Mallory and the old crone, Tutrice. They were back for no good purpose and he wondered what that purpose might be.

CHAPTER THREE

The storm was raging full force. Vanessa and Tutrice fought hard to control the horses as they sped through the open gates and up the winding drive to Bloodstone.

Vanessa whipped the team forward, toward the carriage house. She struggled to hold them steady while Tutrice climbed from the covered carriage and pushed herself against the howling gale. Between the two of them they sheltered the horses and carriage, not bothering to unbridle the team.

"Father will see to them." Vanessa had to yell to make herself heard. "Come, let's get inside before we are swept away."

"The storm is fighting against you, my child. It does not want you here," the old Cajun called.

"Be still. I've had enough of your grumbling. Come along."

Their cloaks and skirts billowed out behind them as they made their way slowly up the walkway, under the portico, onto the wide, sagging front veranda. The pillars supporting the second-story balcony were uneven and weak-looking. Their paint had peeled away long ago, leaving them naked and vulnerable to the terrible winds. They, like the house itself, looked tired and weary.

Vanessa stood for a moment staring at the extent of deterioration. It was as if she were seeing her beloved Bloodstone for the first time. It was not the lovely, stately old mansion she'd left five years ago. It was old and creaky and falling into ruin. It seemed impossible that such a change could take place within the short span of five years.

She refused to dwell on such morbid thoughts. If the house were in need of repair, she would see that it was repaired. She gathered her hood tighter around her head and her cloak about her shoulders and went toward the front door. The wind was blowing so hard it made it difficult for her to see. She groped for the door handle but her hand touched nothing but rough wood. She backed away slightly and saw that the door was boarded over.

"You must not go inside that house," Tutrice warned.

"Be quiet, I say. It's boarded over. Why?"

"They are no longer here, child. You must have known as much."

"Of course they're here. Where else would they be?" She reached out to grab hold of a corner of one of the boards.

"You must not uncrate your own coffin."

"I said, be still," Vanessa hissed, raising her hand as though to strike the old woman. Tutrice did not cower; Vanessa would never strike her, she knew.

"Help me," Vanessa said as again she tried to pull away the boards nailed across the door.

"I will not be a party to this," Tutrice said. "I cannot help you. I will not be responsible."

Vanessa said something angry, but Tutrice did not hear; it was lost in the storm. Frantically Vanessa began tugging at the edges of the boards. One by one they finally came away and were caught up by the wind and carried away.

Finally, the last board came free and Vanessa tried the latch, but it did not move. The door was locked.

She snatched her traveling bag from Tutrice and rummaged inside it, searching. Her fingers touched upon the hard, cold metal of her latch key. She pulled it out.

"No," Tutrice said as Vanessa inserted the key into the lock. "You will never leave once you step inside. You will be a prisoner, like before."

Vanessa gave the key an angry twist. She pushed down on the handle and the door swung easily upon its hinges.

Bloodstone engulfed her the moment she took a step over its threshold. The interior of the house was as quiet as a tomb. Even the raging storm seemed to refuse to cross the sill and intrude upon the deadly calm that hung like a pall over the inside of the old mansion.

"Bloodstone," Vanessa said in reverence, staring at the graceful staircase that curved in a perfect crescent. The storm that raged outside did not stir a single prism of the massive chandelier. Unlike the neglected exterior, the house inside looked as clean and lovely as ever. The marble floors were polished. There wasn't a speck of dust or a stain of neglect anywhere to be seen. The reception hall was as new and bright as it must have been when it was first constructed.

Tutrice remained on the threshold, her cloak and skirt streaming out into the night.

Vanessa took another step deeper into the house. "Father!" she called, looking up toward the top of the staircase. "Father, it's me, Vanessa. I've come home."

She called several more times, but each time was met with the same ominous, almost unearthly silence. With a shrug of annoyance she set down her traveling case and whirled to face the open door. "Get yourself in here," she yelled at Tutrice.

Reluctantly Tutrice took a step toward her, then another. With a deep sigh of resignation she stepped over the threshold. The moment the wind handed her over to Bloodstone, her cloak and skirts fell limp. She sagged and let the tears run unchecked down her wrinkled old face. Slowly, reluctantly she pushed the door shut.

A clock ticked somewhere in the dark recesses of the hall. To Vanessa it was ticking backward in time—back to the year when she was eighteen and standing as she was now, looking fondly at the home she loved so dearly. Then she had looked at it through tears of farewell. She had run away from Bloodstone, away from her weak, distant mother, from her indifferent, uncaring father. She had listened to Tutrice and to her heart and she had allowed her emotions to rule her senses. And so, she had fled.

Without turning, Vanessa asked Tutrice, "Why did I leave all this? For what?"

"You know why," Tutrice answered, almost in a monotone.

"It was you who urged me to run after him."

"No, I merely told you to go away, to go away from this accursed house."

"Stop saying that." Vanessa put her hands over her ears. "Bloodstone is not accursed. It is our home."

"It is your grave." Tutrice shouldered past Vanessa and disappeared through a door tucked under the curving staircase.

"Old fool," Vanessa yelled as the door shut.

Suddenly a man appeared at the head of the stairs. "Vanessa?" he said. "Vanessa, is that you?"

"Father! Oh, Father!" She ran up the steps and threw herself into his arms.

It was not a comfortable embrace, however—they had not been accustomed to embracing. After a moment, she stepped back and looked him up and down.

"You're looking so well," she said, but her father looked far from well. "And Mother? Is she well?"

Her father motioned to a door that stood partly open. "She is in the sitting room." He gave a little chuckle. "You know your mother. She never changes."

But her mother too had changed. Hester Mallory sat before a fireless hearth calmly working on a bit of embroidery. She glanced at Vanessa. She did not smile.

"Hello, Mother. I've come home."

"Yes." Hester gazed at her daughter for a moment, then returned her attention to the needlework in her lap.

Vanessa looked from her mother to her father. "You don't seem surprised at seeing me," she said, forcing the pitch of her voice higher in order to give it a more cheerful lilt. "It has been five years, you know."

"We know," her father answered. "Of course, we are overjoyed at seeing you." He paused. "They told us you drowned."

There was no emotion in his voice. The words came out flat and stiff.

"Me? Drowned?" She suddenly laughed gaily.

Jeremiah nodded gravely. "Five years ago. You and Captain...." He fumbled for a name, but none came to him.

"I'd prefer his name remain unspoken," Vanessa said quickly.

Her mother looked up from her sewing. Their eyes met and locked briefly. After a moment, Hester Mallory looked back down to her embroidery.

"It was a mistake," Vanessa said. "I've come home to start anew. Tutrice and I...."

"Is Tutrice here, with you?" her father asked. He looked strange. His eyes widened, his lips trembled slightly.

"Yes, downstairs. Oh, I left the horses hitched to the landau."

"Everything will be taken care of."

For an uncomfortable moment they just stood looking at each other. "Why is the house boarded up?" Vanessa asked.

"Boarded up?"

"Yes. I had to rip away the boards in order to unlock the front door."

Jeremiah looked toward his wife. "Hester? Were you aware of this?"

"Yes," she said, drawing thread over a design on the linen.

"Please tell me why."

"You forget, Jeremiah. The front door is never used anymore."

Jeremiah cleared his throat. "Yes, yes, of course," he stammered. "I forgot."

"Never used?" Vanessa said, again frowning in confusion. "May I ask why?"

"Bloodstone is very old," her father told her. "It will fall around our heads one day."

"Surely it can be repaired." Vanessa looked around at the lovely, sparkling sitting room. Everything in the room was polished and new looking. The heavy velvet portieres cascaded gracefully from the tops of the French windows. The rugs and furniture were in perfect condition. The upholstery seemed unworn and fresh, the colors vivid and bright.

Her father made a helpless gesture. "Let it fall," he said.

Vanessa whirled on him. "What are you saying? Let Bloodstone fall? You can't let Bloodstone fall into ruin. I won't permit it."

Slowly his eyes moved to meet hers. "It is of no consequence now," he said.

"Of no consequence? You must be mad!" She suddenly realized that something was terribly wrong; something had happened during her five-year absence, something dire. "What happened?"

"Happened?" her father asked innocently. "Nothing. Everything."

"Please explain."

Jeremiah looked away and glanced at Hester. She looked up at him briefly, then back at her sewing.

"There is nothing to explain," Jeremiah told Vanessa.

"There is everything to explain. Bloodstone is gradually falling to pieces on the outside. Why have you allowed it to deteriorate outwardly while inside it is more immaculate than ever?"

"One does not live on the outside of a house," Hester put in without looking up.

Vanessa stared at her. In all her years she'd never known her mother to enter any discussion. She was stunned for a moment. "You're making no sense. I demand to know what has happened since I left."

Tutrice, standing in the doorway, said, "You will learn everything soon enough." She nodded to Jeremiah, then to Hester. "We will stay in the west wing as usual," she told them.

"Of course," Jeremiah answered.

"Come along, child," Tutrice said to Vanessa. "You're tired."

Vanessa's eyes flashed with annoyance. "I am not tired... nor am I hungry...nor am I cold," she snapped. "Leave me be, Tutrice. Why must you hover over me?"

"Suit yourself, girl." The old crone nodded again and started to leave.

"Wait, Tutrice," Jeremiah called.

The old woman turned back and stood waiting.

Jeremiah hesitated. After the pause, he straightened himself and squared his shoulders. "I know Vanessa will not tell us, so I will ask you. What of this man, this sea captain. Is he dead?"

Tutrice shook her head slowly.

"I protest. I forbid you to speak of him," Vanessa fumed.

"No," Tutrice said. "He is not dead. He abandoned her."

Hester's needle pricked her finger. She gave a tight little gasp and stuck the pricked finger into her mouth.

"So," Jeremiah sighed, "it is not finished."

"No, it is not finished," Tutrice said solemnly.

CHAPTER FOUR

The merciless winds continued to whistle and moan, lashing out at everything in their path. Bloodstone stood strong and unbending against the fury of the storm. Yet inside the huge old house there was an eerie calm, like in the eye of a hurricane. Nothing moved, no sound echoed throughout the still rooms and corridors.

Vanessa lay on her wide bed. A smile played lightly on her lips. Her dream was beginning. She was with him and she was happy again. But her smile faded when she saw his eyes grow cold. He mouthed the same words and left her standing high on a cliff overlooking the sea. Below her she saw his ship making ready. Its blood-red sails were hoisted. The captain took his place on the deck; the anchor was raised.

The massive ship moved slowly out toward the distant horizon. A storm was brewing, but the captain didn't seem to care. He nosed his ship, directly into its threatening force. Vanessa watched as the ship grew smaller and smaller. She began to cry, leaning into the wind, trying to catch a last, lingering glimpse of him. The storm grew wilder. Something tugged at her and then without knowing how, she found herself falling down into the icy-cold waters far below.

A scream caught in her throat and she sat bolt upright in the bed. She sat there for several minutes before opening her eyes. When at last she did open them, she felt disappointment. She had hoped that being at Bloodstone would make her dream a reality, but the room was cold and empty and he was gone...gone back to the sea he loved more than her. Why had he spurned her and returned to the sea without her? She knew well the old prophecy that was scrawled so eloquently in the Bible downstairs. She knew it by heart.

"Bloodstone, bloodstone, out of the sea,
Only with that can true love be.
Justice will fall with bloodstone bright
When light will be dark and days will be night;
When life will be death and death will be life,
Then, vengeance will rest with bloodstone and wife."

She had found the bloodstone on his hand. He'd come from the sea. It was all so perfect. Why, then, didn't she get the true love promised her?

Tutrice, of course, scoffed at the prophecy. Tough Tutrice scoffed at everything, Vanessa reminded herself.

Vanessa threw off the covers and got out of her bed. In the light of the dwindling fire she watched her reflection in the shuttered windowpanes. A sudden far and indistinct noise came from somewhere inside Bloodstone. Something fell and crashed to the floor below her. She snatched up her night robe and went to investigate.

The stairs were cold and drafty. A sliver of light shone through the doorway under the staircase, the door through which Tutrice had disappeared earlier.

"Tutrice," Vanessa called softly.

No one answered.

"Tutrice," she called again, walking toward the door. She pushed it open. The door opened onto a large, empty room. A single light burned on a lone table. Vanessa went across the room and opened a door she knew led into the kitchen and pantry area.

Tutrice was sitting at a long, oval table that took up the entire center of the kitchen. The light from the fire played on her wrinkled face, making her look not unlike some ghostly specter. She was huddled over some objects scattered on the tabletop before her. The old woman's eyes were closed, her hands clasped as though in prayer. On the floor beside her Vanessa saw the shattered fragments of a large earthenware bowl. Whatever the bowl had contained was spilled all over the tiles. At first glance Vanessa thought it to be blood.

"What are you doing?" Vanessa demanded.

Tutrice did not move. She sat with her head lowered. Her lips moved but she did not speak. Finally she opened her eyes and continued to look down at the tabletop, studying the objects scattered before her.

"I conjure you," Tutrice moaned. "I conjure you that you forthwith appear. Show yourself, oh dark and mighty master. Show yourself before me in fair and human shape without deformity or ugliness so I will not be afraid. Show yourself. Show yourself now."

"Stop it," Vanessa said, stamping her foot. "Stop it, I say."

But Tutrice stayed as she was. "I conjure you by him to whom all creatures are obedient," she moaned. "The elements have been spilled. The mortal mantle has been broken so that you may come through to me."

"Tutrice! I forbid this nonsense."

Still, Tutrice remained in her trance. "The sea runs back, the fire grows higher, the earth trembles in anticipation of you. Come. Come you in the name of Adonaiu Zabaoth, Adonaij Amiorem."

Vanessa's rushed over to the table and with a wild move of her arm swept all of the objects from the table, flinging them in every direction. She grabbed Tutrice by the shoulders and shook her hard. "I've forbidden you to do this," Vanessa shouted. "How dare you go against my orders."

Tutrice merely sat, numb and unhearing. Gradually she roused herself, turned her head slowly. "Go to bed, child. Leave me to my work."

"No. What are you doing? I demand to know."

Tutrice shrugged indifferently. "I am merely looking for

information," she said.

"Information? What information?"

"About Clarissa. You know Clarissa?"

"Clarissa? Our cook? Of course I know her."

"She is dead," Tutrice said. "She is dead but is not at rest. I was asked to try to find out why she is not at rest."

"I'll have none of that black-magic nonsense in this house. I've told you before, Tutrice. I will not tell you again. I detest this foolishness."

"You detest it because you are afraid of it."

"I detest it because it is stupid. The dead are dead."

Tutrice shook her head. "No," she said. "The dead are never far away from us. They are always here. We have but to reach out and they will be with us again."

"I will not have this mumbo-jumbo practiced here. I will not have it, Tutrice, and I will not warn you of it again. Now go to bed."

To Vanessa's amazement, Tutrice threw back her head and began to cackle. "To bed, to bed. Do you find comfort in your bed, my pet?"

Vanessa raised her hand to strike. Tutrice's eyes bored into her and she froze with hand upraised. Tutrice was not smiling.

"Beware, child. Do not threaten. I know everything. I can only profit you if you will believe in me."

Vanessa found herself trembling. "Sometimes you make me very angry, Tutrice." Then without any warning she buried her face in her hands and began to sob without knowing why.

"There, there, child. Do not weep. I am an old and difficult woman. Like the zebra, I cannot change my stripes. I must do what I am meant to do. I only wanted to help Carl, not disobey you. I promised I would help the poor man."

"Help Carl?" Vanessa sobbed, trying hard to stem her tears.

"He asked me to find Clarissa, his wife. He misses her and knows I have the power to communicate." Tutrice took Vanessa's hand. "I did not mean to hurt you by going against your wishes. I thought you were fast asleep and with him."

Vanessa choked on a sob. She suddenly felt angry instead of sad. She glowered at the old Cajun woman. "Do you find pleasure in tormenting me with reminders of him?"

Tutrice shook her head. "Your moods change with the wind. I do not torment you without reason. You should not be afraid to speak his name or to let mention of him be made. Simply because your stars did not coincide does not mean you should be afraid. It was not meant to be because he was not the right one."

Vanessa's anger went as quickly as it had come. "Oh, Tutrice," she sighed, letting her beloved's face take form in her mind. "Why did it all end as it did? He was as the prophecy predicted. He was the bloodstone from the sea."

"No, you are wrong. He was not the bloodstone from the sea. Something was not right or it would never have ended, or begun," she said.

"But the prophecy in the Bible...."

"He was not the one to fulfill that prophecy. Oh, I too wished it had been so. I, more than you, wished this to come about, but it was not right. We must wait. But I do not think Bloodstone is where we are to wait."

"Why do you hate this house so much?"

"Hate it?" She paused, as though weighing carefully what she intended to say. "I have tried to protect you from Bloodstone because you do not belong here. And I had hoped you would learn that before it was too late."

"Of course I belong here."

Tutrice merely shook her head. "Oh, well, you are here now and here you must stay, I suppose."

"Yes, Tutrice, I must stay. I should never have left."

Tutrice smiled at something that gave her a secret pleasure. "Ah, if only it had worked out differently. If only he had been the one, all this would be changed now and the Bible would read true."

Vanessa knit her brows together. "Read true?"

"It is not what it seems. Things seldom are, you know."

Without anger Vanessa said, "Do you never speak plainly? Why must you always make riddles? Can't you tell me in straight, uncomplicated language the explanation of the prophecy? Please, Tutrice, tell me."

"The prophecy, the prophecy," Tutrice scoffed. "I wish it had never been written." Suddenly her eyes widened and she cringed and clamped her hand over her mouth. She stared about her, cowering, as if expecting some unseen force to punish her for what she'd said.

Vanessa tried not to let herself get annoyed, for she knew how futile it was to try to get Tutrice to speak of the poetic prophecy in detail. But perhaps it was for the best that she did not dwell on the prophecy; it only made her think of him and the bloodstone, which made her unhappy.

"Well, if you won't speak of the prophecy, then tell me of Clarissa. When did she die? Was she very old? In the five years I've been away, I remember her but slightly."

"No, Clarissa was not old, just weary and ready." Tutrice got up and started searching the room for the articles Vanessa had swept off the table. One by one she took them up and brought them back. "Clarissa is in that limbo world where she must wait."

"Wait? For what?"

Tutrice shrugged as she placed the articles into a pattern. "When death touches you, you only stay dead for a while," she explained. "Clarissa is in that temporary death. She will assume her proper place soon. Until then no contact can be made with her. She is dead, as we know death to be. But after her prescribed period of rest is ended, she will be able to communicate."

"You always talk gibberish. I can never make head or tail of what you say."

"It is because you do not hear rightly."

Without realizing what she was saying—for it was as if someone else was speaking for her—Vanessa said, "Tell me the story of the bloodstone again."

Tutrice laughed softly. "No, you are too old for such silly

tales."

"Please, Tutrice. I want to hear it again."

"But I've told you the tale a thousand times."

"Then make this the last time," Vanessa pleaded. "Please, Tutrice. I don't know why, but it suddenly seems very important to me to hear the story once more." She knelt at the old woman's side and put her head in Tutrice's lap. "Tell me about the bloodstone."

Tutrice stroked her hair, smoothing out the long, silky strands. "Very well," she said, "if it is so important. But remember, it is a child's story and you are no longer a child; you are too old for such things, so this will be the very last time." Tutrice paused, formulating the childish tale in her head. She took in a deep breath and began.

"Long, long ago a handsome young sea captain sailed into a strange harbor," she said. "He met with an old man of whom he asked directions as to where the captain might find a night's lodging. The old man told him of an inn and the captain, to express his thanks, invited the old gentleman to come and drink a tankard of ale with him.

"The old man grew to like and trust the handsome young seaman and, confident that he would not regret his trust, confided that he had a beautiful daughter whom he'd kept sheltered from the world. He invited the sea captain to his home to dine.

"The captain accepted and that evening he was surprised to see the magnificent home in which the old man lived. Once inside, the captain met the young daughter. She fell instantly in love with him.

"The captain, being a man of the world, was more interested in the fabulous bloodstone the young maid wore on a chain about her neck. He couldn't keep his eyes from it; the old man and the maid thought the young sea captain's ardent interest was in the girl herself.

"The captain devised a plan to steal the wonderful gem. He succeeded in getting the old man intoxicated and while the old gentleman was in a stupor the scoundrel captain seduced the young maiden and robbed her of her jewel."

"In the morning the maiden, mad with love, ran after her beloved captain. She raced to the harbor just as his ship was leaving port. Unable to be with him, she threw herself into the sea. The young captain, filled with guilt for what he'd done, leaped from his ship in order to save the girl's life.

"He reached her in time; and when he looked into her eyes he knew that he could not live without the maiden's love. He put the bloodstone back around the girl's neck. But the bloodstone had an evil curse on it and the curse added weight to the stone. It was so heavy it pulled the maiden down into the depths of the sea.

"The captain tried to save her but she slipped from his grasp. Rather than face life without his beloved, the young man let himself drift down into the waters so that he might be united with his love in death.

"He found his beloved. The bloodstone lighted his path downward. When he touched her lifeless body a strange and wonderful thing happened. Their love for each other buoyed them up.

"The old man, standing on the shore, saw them rise from the sea and stand beside each other on board the departing ship. He shouted a curse that never again would the captain be permitted to set foot on dry land until both his daughter and the bloodstone were restored to him, but the man and the woman paid no attention to him. To this day, it is said, the old man searches in vain for his lost daughter and the magnificent bloodstone."

Vanessa suddenly stirred and looked up into Tutrice's face. "Is that the meaning of the poem in the Bible? Was my great-great grandfather that old man?"

Tutrice huffed. "No, of course not. I've told you a hundred times that the prophecy has nothing to do with my child's story."

Vanessa put her head back into the old woman's lap. "I believe I'm that girl and that I lost my sea captain somehow and that I must find the bloodstone and him and return them both here to my father's house."

"You talk nonsense. Get off to bed, child and let me get back to my business with Clarissa."

Vanessa got up and went toward the fire to warm herself. "I'll find him one day," she said, more to herself than to Tutrice. "And when I do I shall bring him here and we will be happy forever and forever." She repeated the words of the poem:

"Bloodstone, bloodstone, out of the sea
Only with that can true love be."

She frowned. "'When life will be death and death will be life.' What does that mean, Tutrice?"

Tutrice grunted. "Who knows. It was written a long, long time ago. No one knows what it means."

Vanessa eyed her accusingly. "You know. Tell me."

"Nonsense. I know nothing."

"You know, Tutrice, ever since I can remember you have been with Bloodstone and me. You have never in all that time spoken to me about yourself or your own family...where they came from...who they were. Tell me about them."

To Vanessa's surprise, Tutrice began to laugh. "Never before have you wondered about old Tutrice. I am glad to see you are growing up and can now think of others rather than only yourself." She continued to fool with the objects on the table. "And now I should tell you that in the morning you must go into the village and be about your father's affairs. Won't they be surprised!"

"And what have I to do there?"

"Talk to old Simon Caldwell. He will advise you, and if not Simon, then to Noah Bingham."

"Advise me? Advise me about what?" Vanessa asked.

It was as though Tutrice hadn't heard her. "The storm will blow out to sea now and we must begin our search again."

"Searching again, for what?"

"For your young sea captain and for the bloodstone, of course."

"Don't tease me, Tutrice."

The old woman laughed again and began ladling some horrid-looking substance into a bowl. Vanessa watched, this time with a great deal of interest. Tutrice carried the bowl over to the table and closed her eyes.

"I summon you, spirits of the dead," Tutrice said in a loud voice, "and thee who rules the spirits of the dead, and he who guards the barriers of the stream of Lethe, and he who doles out magic spells and chants a conjuration to appease or compel the fluttering ghosts. Clarissa, hear me!"

Suddenly Tutrice smashed the bowl down on the floor.

CHAPTER FIVE

Vanessa did not dream any more that night. When she awoke she attributed this to her having gone into the library to the opened Bible and recited the words of the poetic prophecy over and over again. It seemed to lift her spirits for some reason she could not explain.

She'd read the poem time and time again and never before saw more than superficial meaning in the words. Now it was different. Perhaps it was her talk with Tutrice in the kitchen. Perhaps it was her having returned home. Perhaps it was Bloodstone itself.

Something had happened to her. She didn't know rightly what, but something was very different this morning. There seemed to be hope in the air. The blind determination that had brought her back to Bloodstone was no longer nagging at her. It wasn't a feeling of determination that goaded her on; it was more a feeling of knowing. She had no fears of failure now. She did not feel plagued with frustration. She *knew* she would find the man with the bloodstone on his hand. It was as if a new vista had opened up during the night.

She threw back the coverlet and looked at herself in the mirror over the dressing table. She even looked different this morning. Her eyes seemed brighter, her complexion younger, smoother. Her hair had a glossier, more brilliant shine and her smile was graceful and relaxed and most attractive.

She hummed as she bathed and dressed, donning one of her loveliest, most flattering dresses. She tied her hair with ribbons and pinched a deeper red into her cheeks, although it hardly made a difference in the color already there. She was happy to be alive, happy to be home, happy to have another day beginning.

The breakfast room was empty. Vanessa passed through to the pantry and eventually the large kitchen. Tutrice was fumbling around near the open hearth. When she heard Vanessa's steps she straightened and nodded a morning greeting. Vanessa put her arms around the old woman and hugged her tight.

"Good morning, dear Tutrice," Vanessa said gaily. "Isn't it wonderful to be alive and home again?"

"Alive? Home? You are as alive as you were yesterday, and you were home yesterday. Why do you think things are different today?"

"Oh, Tutrice, don't be so glum. I feel so happy, so marvelous. I don't think even your gloominess could change that."

"The storm is passed. Perhaps the new day has brought you new hope."

"No, Tutrice. I no longer have to hope. I will merely wait. It will all come to be, just as I wish it to be."

"So, finally you are beginning to understand."

"I don't want to understand; I don't have to. I'm content just to be alive and let fate take care of the rest."

"You did not dream last night?"

"I'm done dreaming."

"That is well—but be wary of your new-found freedom."

"Again you talk in riddles, Tutrice, why don't you ever just say what is on your mind."

"It is that you do not listen, or do not wish to listen. But soon you will understand what you must do."

"Tell me."

"There is Bloodstone first to be thought of. You must get yourself prepared to put things right with Bloodstone."

"I'll speak with Father after breakfast."

"No, not him. Your father cannot do anything, not yet. In time he will help, whether he wishes to or not."

"More riddles." Vanessa went to the big door that led outside and threw it open. Sunlight poured into the room. "Oh, Tutrice. You were right. The storm has gone. And today is meant for fun and laughter."

"And love?"

"Yes, and love." They both laughed.

The door swung open and Jeremiah Mallory appeared. His somber expression seemed to pale the brilliant sunlight.

"Good morning, Father," Vanessa said. "See, the storm has passed."

"You should keep the door closed," he said. "It makes a draft in the house. You know how susceptible your mother is to drafts."

"Forgive me, Father. I forgot." She pulled the door shut. The room was suddenly so cold and so dark, the feeling of being trapped came over her—trapped in her own house.

Tutrice paid no attention to either Vanessa or Jeremiah, but Vanessa saw Tutrice's eyes shift from time to time in Jeremiah's direction. It was as if she were on guard, waiting for something that might happen.

Vanessa forced herself to smile at her father. "Tutrice and I were just talking about Bloodstone, Father. I thought I might go into Skull Point and arrange for repairs to the outside."

"That won't be necessary," he said. "I will take care of it in due time."

"It should be done now," Tutrice put in without looking up.

Jeremiah did not answer her.

"Please, Father," Vanessa said. "I would so like the house to be as it was. You needn't bother with any of the work. I'll attend to everything."

She expected to get an argument, but her father merely nodded and said, "Very well, if that is what you wish." He turned to leave but hesitated and looked back over his shoulder at her. "But your mother must not be disturbed by the workmen. I won't tolerate any of them in the house. She's not as strong as she could be."

"There won't be any need for them to come inside. The interior seems in perfect condition; and I will caution them to be as quiet as possible while they work."

Jeremiah nodded again. He left the room. Vanessa looked at Tutrice. "What's wrong? He doesn't seem to care about Bloodstone. Why? What happened while I was away? I know something happened, but what?"

"Don't bother about your father," Tutrice said. "I've heard he has not been well. People say he thought you drowned and gave up living."

"But I'm home. Surely that should make him happy."

"Perhaps your return was too late." Tutrice came over to her and put a withered arm around her shoulders. "Don't fret about it, my baby. Bloodstone is your concern now. I am sure your father will not interfere with anything you wish to do."

Vanessa wondered what secret existed between Tutrice and her father. Whatever had happened during Vanessa's absence was undoubtedly known to Tutrice.

It was too beautiful a day to wonder about such things, however. She donned a cloak and bonnet, at Tutrice's insistence, and would not hear of Tutrice's offer to chaperone. Once she was outside and saw Bloodstone's crumbling exterior, her heart became heavy. She stood at the back of the house looking up at the sagging shutters, the missing clapboards. She tried to make a mental calculation of the extent of deterioration, but the project seemed too enormous.

"Good morning, miss," a man said as he doffed his hat and smiled at her.

She looked around in surprise. She'd never seen the man before.

"I'm Carl, the stablemaster," he told her. "I heard you were back, Miss Vanessa. Welcome home."

She thanked him but her mind was suddenly on last night and Tutrice's efforts to conjure up this man's dead wife. "I don't remember you, Carl."

"No, miss. I wasn't at Bloodstone when you went away." He

bowed slightly to her and walked away.

Something about the man made her uncomfortable, though. She walked around the side of the mansion and out onto the north terrace, a wide, tiled platform on the very edge of a cliff that fell leisurely down to the sea. Below the marble balustrade edging the terrace stood wave after wave of pines, smelling warm and spicy after the lashing storm. She heard birds twittering and a cool breeze drifted over her, teasing her hair. As far as she could see the ocean stretched out, calm and shimmering. It was an enchanting view.

Vanessa sighed. It was wonderful to be back; she'd never leave Bloodstone again. She stepped onto the path that would eventually take her to Skull Point. The path meandered through the Mallory property, eventually reaching the edge of the bluff and skirted the precipitous cliff for a goodly distance.

She suddenly caught sight of a small sailing boat making ready to leave the shore. Noah Bingham's, she decided. The storm would make the catch a good one, she told herself as she watched Noah and his crew working to bring the boat's nose toward the open sea.

She was unmindful of the soggy, treacherous ground upon which she walked and began to hurry.

The cliff path led toward a grove of dense pine trees. The grove of pines skirted only one side of the path; the other side fell far and sharp down into the sea and the jagged, spear-tipped rocks at the foot of the cliff.

From out of nowhere something or someone shoved hard at the back of her shoulder. Vanessa screamed as her feet slipped out from under her. She fell to the side, toward the cliff and started to roll over the edge.

CHAPTER SIX

Noah Bingham looked up from the line he was securing and thought he saw a figure high up on the edge of the cliff, tumbling around on the very brink. He put his hand up to shade his eyes and saw a woman start to slip over the edge.

* * * * * *

For what seemed an eternity, Vanessa dangled over the edge, clinging to a rock that she grabbed when she fell.

A shadow fell over her, the shadow of a person, she thought, but she was afraid to turn her head to look.

"Help me, please...help me," she cried, but the shadow was gone as suddenly as it had appeared—if it had ever been there.

Vanessa was terrified. She looked at the cliff's edge and saw a small sapling only inches from the rock she was clinging to, but a little higher up. She reached for that and got a firm hold with one hand, then with both hands. She found another rock. Her elbows found solid ground.

Inch by agonizing inch she worked herself gradually upward. Finally she was able to roll onto the surface of the cliff, and safety. She curled herself up into a ball and wept bitterly, aware of nothing but the pounding of her heart and the pain in her muscles.

Gradually she forced herself to concentrate and gather her wits. Someone had pushed her over the cliff...or had she bumped into a low hanging branch that had thrown her off balance?

Whose shape had she seen? Had it been a person or a thing? She buried her face in her hands and shook her head. It had all happened so suddenly, so without warning.

She got unsteadily to her feet. Her legs were numb and shaking. She collected up her skirts and fled back down the path toward Bloodstone, carefully watching her footing and at the same time keeping a wary eye out for branches or people or hands. She dashed through the back door and flung herself into Tutrice's waiting arms. She saw neither her father nor her mother, who were standing in the center of the room.

"Child, what happened?" Tutrice asked hurriedly when she saw Vanessa's torn, muddied skirt, her bruised face and hands.

"Someone tried to kill me," Vanessa sobbed. "Oh, Tutrice, it was horrible."

Tutrice wrapped her arms around the shaking girl and tried to soothe her. "Calm yourself, child. Calm yourself. Here, sit down and try to tell me what happened." She was peering intently into Vanessa's frightened face.

Still ignoring her parents, Vanessa told the story in a choked, sobbing voice. "Someone tried to push me to my death," she finished.

Her mother took a step toward her and placed her hand on Vanessa's shoulder. "Doesn't that seem rather unlikely?" she asked. When Vanessa looked up at her she found her mother was asking the question of Tutrice and not of her.

Vanessa felt the cool touch of her mother's fingers. She shrugged herself free of it and stood up, anger flashing in her eyes. "I tell you someone pushed me over the cliff," she insisted.

"You fell, child," Tutrice said calmly. "I'm sure no one here wants to do you any harm."

"No," Vanessa said sharply, almost in hysterics. "Someone pushed me. I felt their hand at my back. I saw them standing over me waiting for me to fall."

Her father frowned. "But that's absurd, Vanessa. You're imagining it."

"Imagining it?" She held up her hands. "Am I imagining

these cuts and bruises?"

"You fell," her father said, echoing Tutrice's words. "You stumbled in the mud and lost your footing. That path is treacherous after a storm."

"I was pushed, I tell you."

"Nonsense, Vanessa," her mother said. "There isn't a single soul in Skull Point who would harm you. Let Tutrice look after your bruises. Then get out of those muddy clothes and rest yourself. You will feel better after you've calmed yourself down. Later, you will realize that no one was responsible for your fall." She motioned to her husband and they both left the room. Her father turned before the door swung shut.

"Do as your mother says," he told Vanessa. "You'll see things more clearly after you've rested and calmed yourself."

Tutrice got basin and water and began bathing Vanessa's hands. "You don't believe me either, do you, Tutrice?" Vanessa asked.

"It is a rather terrible accusation you make, but if you say you were pushed, then I believe you." She sighed and rinsed the hands clean. "But do not be angry with your parents. You must admit that it is rather unlikely that anyone wanted to do you harm. Hardly anyone knows you are here."

"Carl knows," Vanessa said through clenched teeth.

Tutrice froze. "Carl? Why on earth would Carl want to harm you? He is still grieving for Clarissa; he thinks of nothing else."

Vanessa could not accept that. The thought of Carl made her shiver. "Where did he come from, Tutrice? How long has he been here?"

"Carl came after your father and mother"—she hesitated—"after your father and mother found Bloodstone too much to take care of alone. Clarissa suggested they hire him to look after things. He is a good soul. He would not harm a hair of your head, child. Carl is too deep in grief to think of anything but his beloved Clarissa."

Vanessa remained unconvinced. After she'd gone to her room and had gotten out of her splattered dress, she threw herself across the bed and started to think. If Carl had not been responsible for her near-fatal accident, then who? Tutrice? Impossible. Her father? Her mother? It was difficult to believe, but it was possible that they wanted to be rid of her for some reason or other. Or perhaps others in the village knew she was back. Perhaps Noah Bingham or Simon Caldwell had seen her landau racing through the storm last night. But why would they want to harm her? She was no threat to them.

A tap sounded at the door. "Yes?" she called.

She was surprised to see her mother standing on the threshold. "I came to see how you were feeling," her mother said.

"A bit shaky," Vanessa answered. "I'm fine, otherwise."

Her mother advanced into the room and closed the door softly. "Your father and I were concerned." She did not look at Vanessa. To Vanessa, she did not seem at all concerned. Hester Mallory drifted aimlessly about the room straightening doilies, brushing idly at the tops of commodes and dressers. She went toward the shuttered window and began rearranging the folds of the portieres. "Why have you come back, Vanessa?" she asked, which caused Vanessa to frown. "Surely Tutrice said you should not come back here?"

Vanessa watched her mother. Hester turned and their eyes met. Vanessa felt as though she were looking into a void. "Yes, Tutrice advised that I not come back," she admitted. "But I had to come. I felt that something was waiting here."

"Nothing waits here but death," her mother said.

"Then you do believe someone tried to kill me?"

"No," her mother answered, "I do not believe that. It is not possible that someone tried to take your life."

"But they did."

"I cannot believe that." Her mother turned and started rearranging the various items atop Vanessa's dressing table. "But I did not come here to talk about your accident. I would like to know what happened to you while you were away and why you chose to return to Bloodstone. You found him, did you not?"

"Him?"

"The man who wore the bloodstone on his hand."

"Yes, I found him."

"And he abandoned you."

"Yes," she said in a whisper. "He abandoned me."

"And then what happened? Your drowning. Tell me about that."

"But my drowning was a mistake. I was not drowned, as you can easily see. I have no idea where that unfortunate rumor found its basis. I did not return before this because I felt I should search for him and try to make things right between us." She faltered and let her shoulders droop. "But I never found him again."

"And the bloodstone?" her mother asked.

"The bloodstone? He still wears it."

"Then he was not the right man," her mother said.

"That is what Tutrice keeps saying. Tell me, Mother, what does it all mean? Why is the bloodstone so important to everyone?"

"You should not have come back. You should have kept searching until you found what you must find."

"And what exactly must I find?"

For the first time she saw a glint of light in her mother's eyes. It was a spark of anger. "The bloodstone, of course. It must be returned here to this house or else we will never have peace. Things must be put right, now that we know the truth."

"What truth?"

"The poem in the Bible. Surely you know its meaning now."

"I do not. And I would like someone to tell me."

Her mother was looking at her with amazement. "You mean Tutrice has not told you?"

"Told me what, for heaven's sake? I believe I will go mad."

Her mother turned and started for the door. "But naturally Tutrice would not tell you. You must find it out by yourself."

"No, Mother. Do not leave me. Tell me, please."

"I thought you knew." Her mother left the room and closed the door.

In an agony of frustration, Vanessa went to the window. When she looked down, she saw a small white box with a blood-red ribbon, lying on the ground amid the debris from yesterday's storm.

She ran down the stairs, out of the house, and around to the north terrace, half thinking she would find she had imagined the box—but, no there it was.

She picked it up and undid the bow. Inside, cushioned on red tissue paper, was a small envelope sealed with red wax. She broke the seal and extracted a slip of paper. On the paper was neatly printed, "If you are alive then I must see you. Come to the old covered bridge at eight tonight." There was no signature.

The sun was warm on her back as she stood there looking down at the neatly printed little message. A soft breeze toyed with the paper in her hand. "If you are alive," she reread.

CHAPTER SEVEN

Vanessa knew who had sent it.

She'd almost forgotten Brian McGrath. They had been sweethearts once, but that was a long, long time ago. Vanessa had been seventeen and Brian only two years older.

She laughed to herself as she thought about Brian. She was never in love with him, though many thought so. Brian wasn't from the sea. She'd always had a penchant for the sea. Still, she planned to keep the rendezvous.

* * * * * * *

A full moon was out. Somewhere a dog barked. Then it was silent. Far out in the blackness the sea whispered under a pleasant breeze.

Vanessa walked quickly along the roadway, where tufts of grass muffled her steps. Far ahead she saw the village with its tiny lighted windows and smoking chimneys. The church bell tolled eight times and Vanessa quickened her pace.

Brian mustn't know about the sea captain. She'd have to keep that secret. She'd have to think up some other excuse for having stayed away for five years without letting anyone know of her whereabouts or her doings. She wouldn't give them the pleasure of knowing she'd been abandoned by a man. No one walked away from a Mallory, she told herself.

Before she could think up a likely story, Brian was there, standing at the covered bridge. When he saw her he threw away the long blade of grass he was chewing on and hurried to meet her.

He beamed and took her hands in his. "Oh, Vanessa, you're back. How wonderful you look...as beautiful as ever."

"Aren't you going to kiss me?" Vanessa asked boldly. She turned her cheek. He touched it lightly with his lips.

"Why didn't you write?" he asked. "I've been in misery these past years wondering if I would ever see you again. When we heard you had drowned, my world ended."

Vanessa laughed again. "Oh, Brian, it is good to hear your voice again and to be with you. It has been a long time, hasn't it?"

"Much too long." He pulled her into his arms.

Vanessa resisted and eased herself out of his embrace. "Then you haven't married?"

"Married? Never. I could never marry anyone but you. Where have you been, Vanessa? Why have you tortured me all these years by letting me think you drowned?"

"I don't remember. I think I lost my memory or something. I fell and hurt my head. I don't remember where I've been."

Brian frowned at her. "They said you were dead," he told her. "Is that the accident you speak of?"

"I guess so. I was supposed to have drowned or something, but as you can plainly see, I didn't. Now, tell me about yourself. Tell me about Skull Point."

"Things here are as they have always been."

"What happened at Bloodstone? Why have my parents let it fall into neglect?"

"There was no one to keep it up. After the news of your supposed drowning, your father and mother just stopped caring about life."

"But they're so changed, I hardly recognized my father...and mother isn't at all the same."

Brian stared at her and took a step backward. "You say you had an accident and hurt your head?"

"Yes, I told you that. I lost my memory for ever so long. Then it came back to me and I came home. But I don't want to talk about me. Tell me about my parents, about Skull Point."

"As I said, there's nothing to tell. The town is prospering. Everyone is concerned about the war with the South. There is much talk about a big plant some New York investors want to build here in Skull Point. Everyone is against it. They say it is to be a munitions factory."

"Who cares about a silly old war and a munitions factory? I want to know about...."

"But the factory is terribly important. It might mean the end of our village."

"Would that be such a great loss?"

Brian wondered if this could possibly be the same Vanessa Mallory he'd known before. She was so different. "I must take you home," he said. "It is getting late. You must be tired."

"But you haven't told me anything. You haven't told me about my parents, about Bloodstone."

"Bloodstone is as you see it. As for your parents...did you know, your father deeded over the Mallory lands to the town?"

"My father did what?"

"He deeded the Mallory lands over to the town of Skull Point. Everything except Bloodstone itself."

"Why did he do that?"

"Who else would he leave it to? You were believed drowned. There was no one else, I suppose."

"Why did he deed it over to anyone at all?"

"Someone had to have the properties. It would have reverted to the township legally in any case."

"I'm going home, Brian," she said hurriedly. "I must go home."

Brian hurried to keep pace with her. The soft ground beneath their feet made their walking soundless. They left the edge of Skull Point behind them.

She had all but forgotten that Brian was with her. She was thinking how foolish and stupid her father had been! What had possessed him to turn everything they had in the world over to

Simon Caldwell?

Leaving the lands to Skull Point meant exactly that, too—
Simon Caldwell and his little band of mercenaries that clung to
him like so many parasites. Well, the lands would be returned,
she vowed. She didn't know how she would manage it, but she
would manage it somehow. Tutrice would know a way.

Her steps suddenly faltered. Perhaps Tutrice knew already.
Why hadn't she told her? she wondered.

A shadow moved across the road in front of them. Vanessa
stopped dead in her tracks. She stopped so suddenly Brian
bumped into her in the darkness. "What is it?" he asked, looking
at her with alarm.

She pointed. "There. Someone just darted across the road
and disappeared into those trees."

"I saw no one." He started toward where Vanessa pointed.

She clutched his arm. "No, it may be dangerous."

"Well, we can't stand in the middle of the road all night," he
said, trying to sound unconcerned.

"See, it's nothing," Brian said when they reached the spot
to which Vanessa had pointed. He found himself whispering.
"You're just imagining things, Vanessa."

When they reached the gates to Bloodstone, Brian stopped.
"I can't go any farther," he said.

Vanessa looked at him with surprise. "Why not?"

"It was your father's wish. No one from Skull Point is
permitted to set foot on the Bloodstone estate. These are the
only lands that remain in the Mallory family."

"But you came this afternoon when you left your note."

"I was desperate. I had to see you. You mustn't tell anyone
about that note."

"But I don't understand. Why would my father forbid anyone
from coming onto the property? It is ridiculous."

"No one knows why, but everyone is bound by his wishes.
He made it a condition of his last will and testament."

"His last will and testament!"

"Yes. When they died your father left all the Mallory property to Skull Point and ordered that no person set foot inside Bloodstone or the immediate grounds surrounding it."

Vanessa's eye were as large as saucers. "When they died?"

CHAPTER EIGHT

To Brian's astonishment she threw back her head and laughed. Still laughing, she ran up the drive toward Bloodstone.

Brian kicked a stone out of his way and started slowly back toward the village. Once or twice he glanced over his shoulder. Vanessa had acted so strangely. She must be demented—maybe from that accident she'd mentioned. He wished he had never fallen in love with Vanessa Mallory.

* * * * * * *

Tutrice was sitting quietly in one corner of the kitchen. When she heard Vanessa's laughter she stirred.

Vanessa burst into the kitchen, still laughing. She leaned against the table and tried to catch her breath.

Tutrice folded her thin arms across her scarecrow bosom. "I could use something to cheer me, child. Tell me what you find so amusing," she said.

Vanessa tried to keep from bursting into laughter again. "They're dead, Tutrice. My Parents are dead."

"You find humor in death?"

"Only when I know it isn't true. My father and mother aren't dead."

"Who told you they were?"

"Brian. He must be out of his head. He said father died and left all the Mallory properties to the town—Simon Caldwell, in other words. He said that father's will prohibits any of the villagers to set foot inside Bloodstone. Don't you see how ridiculous it is? Father and Mother are here. We've seen and spoken to them. They can't be dead."

"Ah, but we are," Jeremiah said from the doorway. There was the hint of a smile at his mouth.

"Father," Vanessa said, running to him. "Did you hear what I said?"

He nodded. "For every intent and purpose your mother and I are indeed dead."

"I don't understand."

"We wish to keep the villagers out of Bloodstone. We have our reasons, of course. We want them to believe we are dead."

"But that's ridiculous. How can you make people think you're dead when you aren't? Why would you want to do anything so absurd?"

"We have our reasons."

"Then what Brian said is true. You deeded all our lands to Simon Caldwell."

"We deeded the lands to Skull Point."

"Why? Those properties are as much mine as yours. I'm a Mallory also, remember."

"You were believed drowned. At the time we made the arrangements there was no one else."

"And you and Mother have lived here since like hermits."

Her father nodded.

"But it makes no sense. Why do such a thing?"

"We have our reasons. We are presumed dead. Leave it at that."

"I'll get to the bottom of all this if it is the last thing I do." Vanessa turned angrily and stormed out of the room.

As she hurried across the reception hall, toward the curved staircase she glanced toward the library and saw a flicker of light. A single lamp was burning on the library stand. Beside the lamp was the Bible...the Mallory Bible.

Something drew her to it. She stood looking down at the familiar pages with their beautifully scrolled letters. She felt a compelling urge to turn to the back and reread the poem. Instead, she slammed the covers shut.

She had never seen the Bible closed. Her father had told her that a Bible should always be opened, inviting anyone to read. He used to say the same thing about the lovely pianoforte sitting in the music room; it was never covered; the lid was always raised in invitation to anyone who wished to play.

Now the Bible was closed. Its thick gold-and-jeweled cover glinted in the light of the lamp. There were letters spelled out in seed pearls. The letters did *not* spell "Mallory" as she expected, but another name. She traced the pearls with her finger. *"Justice."*

"Who was Justice?" she asked the empty room.

Suddenly something registered. Quickly she reopened the Bible and flipped back to where the poem was scrawled. There it was, in the poem:

Justice will fall with bloodstone bright.

She read the line slowly. What did it mean? Whose justice would fall with the bloodstone?

Again she closed the Bible and stared down at the word "Justice" spelled out so gracefully in the gleaming, tiny pearls. She knew the meaning of the word well enough. It meant an act, practice, or obligation of rendering to a person that which is his or her due, as in conformity with right, truth, or the dictates of reason.

But who will benefit? she asked herself.

She was so engrossed in the mystery of the poem Vanessa did not hear her mother come into the library. Her mother reached around her and flipped the Bible open again.

"Never close the Bible, dear," Hester said.

"I'm sorry, Mother. It was just an urge.... What does 'Justice' mean?"

"Surely you know its definition."

"Yes, but why is it bejeweled on the cover of our Bible,

instead of our family name?"

"There is a mystery behind the word. It is up to you to unravel that mystery. Come with me. Carl is in the kitchen. He says he has a message for you."

"Carl? With a message for me?"

"He says it is from Simon Caldwell."

"What on earth does Simon Caldwell have to do with me? Brian lost little time advertising my return."

"Don't blame Brian, my dear. Everyone knows. You were seen driving through the storm last night."

Last night suddenly seemed to have been years and years ago. Vanessa had forgotten the storm, the drive through the lashing winds. It was as if she had never left Bloodstone...that she'd been here all those long, strange years.

* * * * * * *

Carl was standing near the back door, hat in hand.

"You have a message, Carl?" she asked.

"That I do, miss. Simon Caldwell sent me. He says for you to come tomorrow. He wants to speak with you, miss. He says if ten o'clock would be convenient he would much appreciate it."

"Tell Simon Caldwell that ten o'clock may not be convenient for me. I will come when I am ready to come. At my pleasure. I am a Mallory. I do not take orders from the likes of Simon Caldwell."

"Yes, miss," Carl said. "I understand." He turned slowly and went out the door.

CHAPTER NINE

In the morning, she took the short way into Skull Point, along the beach. She did not think she would ever summon the courage again to tread that treacherous, winding path at the top of the cliff. The path that had almost meant her end.

It was well past ten o'clock. Simon Caldwell would be furious with her, but still she walked slowly, relishing the sinking softness of the sand, the gentle lapping of the surf, the clusters of rocks scoured white by the sea and sun.

She caught sight of the town and quickened her pace. She wanted to be with people all of a sudden. She made her way carefully through the last pile of rocks and sea kelp, ignoring the buzzing little gnats that infested the slimy sea-grass.

The man was lying half in, half out of the water. With the sun directly in her eyes, Vanessa wasn't sure it was a man at first. It looked as pale and bleached as the sand and the bright sunlight made it difficult to distinguish.

She stopped and stared, not believing her eyes. The man was dressed in tatters that were once some kind of naval uniform. His hair, dark and thick, floated out from his head as the surf lapped in and out, buoying him up, letting him float for a moment, then bringing him back down to rest on the sandy shore.

Her first impulse was to run and cry for help. She didn't move, however. Who was it? she wondered. She took a step or two closer. He lay on his back, his face looking up into the sky. She did not know him.

The murmur of voices made her look up. There, trudging

along the beach was the familiar figure of Noah Bingham and several other men. She waved and ran to meet them.

"Well, Miss Vanessa," Noah said, holding out his hand. "We heard you were back."

She didn't bother with cordialities. "There's a man lying in the surf, over there," she said. "Come quickly. He must have drowned in the storm."

The men exchanged looks.

Then Noah dropped the nets he was carrying. He ran in the direction Vanessa pointed. When Noah ran, the others followed suit.

"Hey, there is a body," one of the men said in disbelief.

Noah knelt down and examined the eyes and the pulse, putting his ear to the man's chest. "He's alive," he announced. "Come on, boys, help me get him over to my place." As the men started to lift him, Noah said, "Easy there, he may have some broken bones. Be careful with him."

"Who is he?" Vanessa asked.

"Never saw him before," Noah said. "Maybe his ship broke up in the storm. He seems to be a sailor of some sort."

They puffed their way up the steep path that cut into the side of the bluff. The way was almost straight up, but it was the quickest route to Noah's house. No one said anything until they were on the top.

"We saw no wreckage on the water," Noah said. "I can't think where the lad came from."

"Lad?" Vanessa hadn't thought of age when she'd studied the man's face, but now as she looked at the head that lolled to one side, bobbing as it was carried on the shoulders of the men, she could see that he was indeed young—no more than her own age—and extremely good-looking. His hair was jet black, his face bronzed and rugged, with a square chin, straight nose, and full, sensuous lips. Although the eyes were closed, she was certain their color would be the same deep blue as the sea. She glanced at his hands, hoping to see a bloodstone ring on his fingers, but his fingers were naked. A tinge of disappointment went through her.

Noah called for his wife when they came within sight of his house. "Ruth!"

She appeared in the doorway. When she saw them carrying their burden she hurriedly put aside her broom and started toward them.

"Get a bed ready, woman," Noah yelled. She turned and rushed back inside the house.

As they neared Noah's property, Vanessa could see damage left by the storm. The Bingham fence was gone, a tree lay across the once well-manicured lawn. One or two shutters were missing and many of the roof tiles had been carried away.

The men carried the man's body into the house. Ruth was there to direct them. Vanessa found herself standing alone for a few minutes, hesitant about pushing her way into Noah's house and into one of his bedrooms. But she wanted to go, she wanted to be with the man she'd fished from the sea. Ruth appeared again almost at once.

"They'll get him out of his clothes and my husband will look him over. I suppose we should send for Doc Smithers."

"I could go."

"No, child. One of the boys will run for him. You come with me into the kitchen and I'll fix you a nice cup of tea. Noah tells me you came across the sailor washed up on the beach."

"Yes, I was on my way to see Simon Caldwell when I saw him lying there."

"Poor dear. It must have given you quite a fright. Sit yourself down, girl, and I'll get the kettle started." She began rattling around at the stove. "To see Simon, you say? I suppose it would be about your dear father's will?"

"Mister Caldwell sent for me. He did not say what he wanted to speak with me about."

Ruth turned and straightened herself. "Simon sent for *you?* The brass of that man. He's gotten very high and mighty since your poor old father passed away."

"I'm not particularly pleased by what my father did," Vanessa said. "They had no way of knowing that I was very much alive."

Ruth gave her an odd look. "Brian's been saying you were hit on the head or something. Poor child, wandering all alone without anyone to take care of you." She paused. "Brian says you don't remember where you were."

Vanessa remembered the game she'd played with Brian, pretending she didn't remember anything. Apparently he'd taken it all very seriously.

"If Simon Caldwell gives you any bother," Ruth said, returning her attention to the kettle on the stove, "You just come over here and speak with Mr. Bingham. Noah will stand up to Simon. He's just about the only man in Skull Point who will."

"I'm sure Mr. Caldwell will give me no bother. I'm quite capable of looking out for myself. But I thank you for the offer."

"Ah, you're a Mallory through and through all right. You sounded just like your old grandfather just then. Now there was a man who took no guff from anyone."

One of the men who helped carry the body up the bluff came out of the bedroom. "Noah's sending me for old Doc Smithers," he said both to Ruth and to Vanessa. "We've got the lad bedded down. He don't look none too good though."

"Then you'd better hurry and fetch the doctor. Get along with you," Ruth said, shooing the man out of the kitchen. He went on the run.

The kettle started to whistle. Ruth fetched cups and saucers and placed them on the table. She put tea leaves into a small white pot, made the tea and put it aside to steep. "Are you going to stay now that you're back?" she asked Vanessa.

"Yes, I believe I will. I intend to fix up Bloodstone. I'm afraid my parents let it fall into wrack and ruin."

"Well, there's plenty of able-bodied young men around who'd be only too anxious to do the work for you—that is, if you can coax them into going up to the house."

Vanessa frowned. "I thought of that. Brian told me about the strange condition my father put on deeding over the land. But I'm sure if I asked them they'd do it without feeling they were going against my father's wishes. He told me he did not object to having the work done just as long as the workmen don't bother my mother with a lot of racket and just as long as they stay outside the house."

Ruth was gaping at her. "Your father told you?" she said.

Vanessa nodded. "My parents were ever so happy to see me return home," she said, watching Ruth Bingham with amusement.

Ruth continued to stare at her. Brian had been right. The girl was quite daft. She turned quickly and began to pour the tea. She saw that her hands were shaking noticeably.

Noah Bingham strode in. Ruth found his presence welcome. She was getting most unnerved by this strange Mallory girl.

"Well, the lad doesn't seem too sound," Noah said. "But we'll wait and see what old Doc Smithers says after he's had a chance to look him over. There was a lot of water in the lungs, but Josh and I managed to get most of it out of him. He'll be a sick boy for a day or so—if he recovers at all, that is."

"I hope you didn't make a mess of my room," Ruth complained, glad to get her mind on something besides the strange Mallory girl.

"Can I see him?" Vanessa asked anxiously, getting to her feet.

"Best let him rest, child. There's nothing to see but the body of a half-drowned young man. Sit, have your tea."

"So you've come back to us, Vanessa Mallory," Noah said, settling himself down on a chair across from her. "We're all pleased to see you, girl."

"Not all of us," Ruth put in, pouring her husband a cup of tea. "I'll be betting that Simon Caldwell won't be too pleased to see her, nor any of that no-good bunch that hangs around him."

Noah picked up his pipe and lit it. "Will you be fighting to get the property back, Vanessa?"

She shook her head. "I'll let Simon control the properties. It's what my father wants me to do."

Ruth and Noah exchanged knowing looks. Noah clamped his

teeth down hard on the stem of his pipe. "When did you talk to your father, child?"

Vanessa gave him a wide innocent stare. "Why this morning... no...yesterday. We talk together all the time."

Noah leaned across the table and took one of her hands in his. "Child, you must understand. Your parents are both dead. You can't have talked to them."

"Oh, but I did," Vanessa said, still innocent, although she wanted to smile. "But I must admit, Father does not look well. He is very drawn looking. And mother is paler than ever."

"Where do you talk to them?" Noah asked.

"Why, at home, of course." The game was getting more and more amusing. "Of course you can't talk with them. Nobody can, except me and Tutrice."

Again Noah glanced at his wife. Ruth tapped her head and made a face.

"Tutrice tells me that Father and Mother are in a state of limbo. They'll be out of it in a short while. Until then, nobody can talk to them. I don't understand why I can communicate. I suppose it's because I'm living inside Bloodstone. They never want to go out of it. They can't, Tutrice tells me, until their period of limbo is ended."

"Limbo," Noah said thoughtfully as he chewed on the stem of his pipe. "I see," he said. She was crazier than Brian had led them to believe, he decided.

"Yes. Tutrice can talk to them because she's living in the house too. She couldn't talk with Clarissa though. She said Clarissa hasn't been dead long enough to enable her to get through the black mist that they must live inside when in limbo."

Now she knew the girl was crazy, Ruth told herself. Clarissa, the old Mallory cook, was in the market this morning. She'd spoken to her. Clarissa didn't work at the Mallory place any longer. The town had set her husband, Carl, up as a kind of watchman over the Mallory house just to be sure it was safe from possible vandals. Yes, poor Vanessa Mallory was quite insane.

"Clarissa, your old cook?" Noah asked. "You say she's dead also?"

"Oh, quite dead. Tutrice tried to reach her, but the mist was too thick. She did reach someone, though. I didn't ask who."

One of the men came out of the bedroom and said, "The lad's coming round, Noah. I just saw his eyes flicker open for a second."

Vanessa was on her feet in an instant. Noah got up and hurried toward the bedroom. Vanessa and Ruth were close on his heels, although Ruth made certain there was a good distance between herself and Vanessa Mallory.

The lad was lying on stark white sheets with a quilt thrown over him. The quilt was tucked up under his chin. The men had managed to dry his hair and Vanessa saw how thick and beautiful it was. The face looked more handsome than it had when first she'd seen it. He looked quite calm and peaceful lying there.

"You'd better fix some broth or something, Ruth," Noah said. "If the lad comes around he'll be wanting something in his stomach."

"Who do you think he is, Noah?" one of the men asked.

"Don't know. He don't look familiar at all."

"If there was a shipwreck we would have seen the flotsam."

"Maybe, maybe not," Noah said.

Vanessa was staring hard into the young man's face. She felt she'd seen him somewhere before, but could not place where. It must have been in a dream, she decided.

"The doctor's coming," Ruth called from the doorway.

Doctor Smithers was a thick little man with heavy glasses and a moustache that curled up at the ends, giving him a pixie look. He leaned over the bed and examined the young man's eyes, then took an instrument out of his black bag and folded back the quilt.

At first she didn't see it. The doctor was blocking her view. She moved to watch. Then she stared. Noah and the other men had managed to undress the seemingly lifeless young man. He was naked beneath the quilt and when the doctor turned back the quilt, his upper torso was exposed.

There, on a string around his neck was the largest, most beautiful bloodstone ring in the world. She stared at it. Everything in her dream came back as vividly as ever. She had seen the stone before. She had seen the very stone on the hand of a man who had boarded a ship with blood-red sails and sailed out of her life. It was the very stone. She was positive of it.

"Bloodstone, bloodstone, out of the sea," she said.

CHAPTER TEN

Simon Caldwell was sitting in front of the general store, flanked by Sam Hastings and Will Wilkins. Between the two heavy-set men, Simon looked dwarfed. His straight black suit made him look thinner than he was. One could tell, however, just by the way Simon sat, which of the three was the most powerful-minded. His back was straight and he held his head tilted slightly upward, giving him a regal look.

"Crazy as a loon, Brian said she was," Will Wilkins said.

"Now, Will," Simon said. "Brian said no such thing. He said she was acting a little odd, that's all. She'd had a head injury. That doesn't mean she's crazy."

He was pleased with himself at his show of tolerance toward Vanessa. He'd never particularly liked the girl—boy-crazy, he'd always thought her to be. It gave him a secret pleasure to stand up for her when all the villagers were now convinced that a madwoman had returned and was living in the Bloodstone house.

"It's after eleven o'clock, Simon. I don't think she's coming."

"She'll come," Simon said with confidence. "She'll come because she'll think I want to talk about her father's deeds. Perhaps she'll not come in answer to my summons, but nevertheless she'll come."

The three of them leaned forward when they saw young Josh Lancey running down the center of the street. He didn't come as far as the general store. He ran into Doc Smither's Office.

"I wonder what that's all about?" Sam said. "Looks like

somebody's sick."

A moment later Josh reappeared with Doc Smithers. They jumped into the doctor's buggy and rode off.

Will and Sam stood up and looked to see which direction they were going. "It looks like they're heading for Noah's place," Will said.

Doc Smithers' buggy seemed to bring the town to life. A dog jumped up from its sleep in the sun and began chasing the buggy, barking excitedly. Several children appeared from out of nowhere and ran after the buggy as well, rolling their hoops faster and faster and squealing with childish glee.

People appeared in doorways, faces in windows. No one had seen old Doc Smithers' buggy move so fast in a long, long time. Something had happened, something exciting. Men and women alike were suddenly streaming into the street, all questioning one another as to the doctor's destination.

"What's going on, Simon?" one of the women called.

Simon sat coolly erect and unruffled by the flurry of activity. He didn't bother to answer her; he let Will Wilkins do that.

"We don't know," Will called to the woman. "Josh ran in like there were devils chasing him. He went straight to the doc's and they both took off. We think they're heading for Noah Bingham's place."

Simon was pleased to remain aloof from the exchange of conversation. Whatever had happened, be it important, he'd know soon enough.

The day was turning hot and Simon felt uncomfortable. He rose from his chair with the grace of a judge dismissing court. "I have things to attend to," he told Will and Sam and when they started to go with him, he waved them off. "If the Mallory girl shows up, I will be at home," he said.

Simon looked neither right nor left. He nodded to those who greeted him, but did not look at them unless they were directly in front of his eyes. He was careful always not to become too familiar with any of the townspeople. That was how he kept their respect, he told himself. He was the head of Skull Point, and the head of any place never mingles with its subjects.

He was annoyed that Vanessa Mallory had failed to keep their appointment. The girl had always been too independent for her own good. A slight frown wrinkled his already wrinkled forehead. He would need Vanessa, however. The use of her name would be valuable. He would have to make her see things his way. As much as he detested the Mallorys, he had to admit the family was well known and extremely powerful. Jeremiah had been a strong supporter of the new governor. The governor was a personal friend of Jeremiah's and the governor was the only man who could grant him what he asked.

"Hello, Simon," Brian McGrath.

Simon hesitated. "Brian," he said, "you've met with Vanessa, I understand."

"Yes, last evening."

"You say she is not well."

"She acted most peculiarly, Simon. She actually laughed at me when I told her of her parents dying."

"And she admits to an accident?"

"She claims she hurt her head and suffered a loss of memory. She says she don't know where she's been these past five years."

Simon thought for a moment then went directly to the point. "Do you still feel the same way about the girl, Brian?"

Brian flushed slightly. Everyone in Skull Point knew how enamored Brian was of Vanessa. He'd always been and everyone thought it was a mutual feeling until Vanessa dashed away in a storm and didn't return until five years had passed.

"I still feel the same about her, Simon."

"Good. Good," Simon answered, still thinking, plotting, scheming. "I would deeply appreciate a favor from you, Brian. Could you communicate with Vanessa and arrange for her to visit me at her convenience." He was swallowing his pride, but he knew he had to. "Something rather important has come up and I will need her help."

"Has it to do with the munitions factory?"

"Yes, as a matter of fact, it does."

"I don't think she'd be interested in helping us with that problem. I told her about it last night and she didn't think it was important."

"Of course it is important. She must take an interest."

"Well, all I can say, Simon, is you'd better see her for yourself. She's changed a lot. She doesn't seem to be interested in anything but that precious Bloodstone she lives in."

Martha Wilkins came running up to where Simon and Brian stood talking. "I just heard the news, Simon," she said breathlessly, beaming with pleasure because she was to be the first to let Simon know what was happening at Noah Bingham's house. "They found a young man washed up on the beach. That Vanessa Mallory girl found him. He's some kind of sailor. They carried him over to Noah's place but Doc Smithers thinks he should be moved here to town where he can keep an eye on him. No one knows who the man is."

"You say Vanessa found him?"

"Yes," Martha went on, still breathless. "And she's making a terrible row. She wants the man taken up to Bloodstone, but the doc won't hear of it. He just told her it was out of the question. Doc insists the man be here in Skull Point."

Simon nodded. "I'll speak to the doctor. Perhaps the patient can be housed in my place. I've the room and the facilities."

Martha Wilkins made her mouth into an oval. "Oh, I think Vanessa would really bellow if she thought the man was going to be placed there, Simon." She leaned close to Simon's ear and cupped her hand around her mouth so Brian wouldn't hear. "I think she's smitten."

Man-crazy, Simon thought. Vanessa had always been that way. Simon turned and started back the way he'd come. Martha and Brian fell in beside him. "I'll wait for Doctor Smithers. If Vanessa is with him I'll just have to force her into listening to reason. Bloodstone is out of the question. It's falling into ruin. There's no one there to care for the sick man. Besides, it would be scandalous to have him lodged with a single woman, scandalous."

"And don't forget Jeremiah's stipulation," Brian said.

"Of course that must be considered too," Simon said. "Jeremiah made it quite clear that no one is to set foot inside Bloodstone...immediate family excluded, of course." Simon wouldn't admit that the latter was the main reason he didn't want the man—whoever he was—taken to Bloodstone. Nothing must be done to endanger the grant deeds. Jeremiah's wishes must be met to the letter.

Simon seated himself on a chair outside Doc Smithers' office. He politely but firmly dismissed Martha and Brian when they offered to sit and wait with him.

Vanessa would have to listen to reason. He needed her help desperately.

It was well into the afternoon before Doc Smithers' buggy returned. Simon was still there in front of the office waiting for him.

"I hear we have a half-drowned stranger amongst us," Simon said as the doctor got down from his buggy.

"Yep, he's a stranger all right. Don't know who he is, Simon, but you're right, he's half-drowned. Oh, I got him to come around. He'll be a little wobbly for a couple of days but he'll be fine in no time." He went into his office. Simon followed him. "We went through his pockets, but there isn't a single thing that tells us anything about him."

"I've been waiting to offer that the man be housed at my place," Simon said. "You know I have the room and facilities and plenty of servants to give him proper attention."

"That's darned nice of you, Simon, I suppose he would be more comfortable there. He'll need a nurse, I think."

"You can arrange for that," Simon said. "There's plenty of room in my house."

Doc Smithers scratched his chin. "Vanessa would have liked to take the man to Bloodstone, but I told her she had to think of the wagging tongues. She won't take kindly to the man's going to your place." He laughed. "Oh, she spat and stammered and yelled when I put my foot down, but I stood up to her. She's a little crazy, that one. Never saw the likes of the way she was carrying on."

"Where's the man now?"

"They're carrying him up from Noah's place. Ruth wanted to be rid of him. She said he was a bad omen." He chuckled again. "But you know Ruth. If it means extra work she's against it."

The door suddenly burst open and Vanessa, flushed with anger, strode in and faced Doc Smithers squarely. "I told you I wanted that man taken to Bloodstone. They're on their way here with him now."

"Hello, Vanessa," Simon put in, but she ignored him completely.

"Now, Vanessa," Doc Smithers said kindly. "I explained to you that it would not be proper for you to take a single young man into your house. You've no one to care for him except yourself, which would be unseemly."

"Tutrice could care for him. And my parents are there. Between us we could look after him very well."

The doctor and Simon exchanged looks. The doctor shook his head. "It just wouldn't be right, girl. Think of what the town would say. It would be unthinkable. The only thing your old guardian knows about treating people is that voodoo stuff she's always been practicing. No, I'm sorry, Vanessa, it is out of the question. I will not have it. The man is being taken to Simon Caldwell's."

Vanessa, for the first time, acknowledged Simon's presence by turning and glowering at him. "Simon Caldwell's? Never. The man is coming with me."

"Now, Vanessa," Simon said softly. "Contain yourself, child. If the man needs care, who in Skull Point has more room or more people to attend to him than I? He will be well cared for. After all, it will only be a matter of a few days before he is up and around. At that time we will let the man make up his own mind as to where he wishes to be lodged. Perhaps he may not wish to remain in our town at all."

"He must remain."

The two men were looking at her oddly. Brian had understated the condition of her mentality, Simon thought. The woman was raving mad.

"Vanessa, calm yourself," Doc Smithers said. "I cannot understand why you are taking on so about some strange bedraggled seaman who happened to get himself washed up on our beach. You are behaving most peculiarly."

Simon glanced at him, wondering if he'd missed the current gossip about Vanessa being demented.

"If I am acting peculiarly, it is for my own good reasons. I do not have to discuss my family's business with you or anyone else."

"But, my dear child, what on earth does your family have to do with this strange man? Do you know who he is?"

"No. Yes."

"Vanessa," Doc Smithers said. "Try and control yourself. Try to see things our way. The man is unconscious. There may be complications brought on by his near drowning that we will not know about for a day or two. His lungs may have been infected. He may die. We don't know and we can't know until he comes around. It would be most impossible for me to make continued treks to Bloodstone. And if I did come, I would not be able to enter the house because of the condition of your father's will."

"Of course you could enter the house. What's to prevent you?" Vanessa said angrily.

"You know the provisions of your father's will. He forbade anyone to set foot on the property, let alone in the house itself."

"My father's will...my father's will," Vanessa said impatiently. "How could my father leave a will when he isn't dead?"

Doc Smithers had indeed heard the rumor about Vanessa's mental state. Vanessa's remark made it all too clear that what the people were saying about her was true.

"Go home, child, and try to collect yourself. We'll house the man at Simon's. I'm sure Simon will have no objections whatsoever to your visiting the man as often as you like."

"No objections at all," Simon agreed.

Vanessa stood there fuming, looking from one to the other. The man she'd found on the beach had the bloodstone ring in his possession, and he was from the sea. It couldn't be clearer to her, he and his precious bloodstone had somehow to be returned to Bloodstone manor.

Well, if she could not have the man and his stone immediately, then she would just have to bide her time until she could.

"Very well," she said finally. "Have the man taken to Simon's. I will visit him as often as I like. And the man is not to leave Skull Point without express permission from me, is that understood?"

Doc Smithers continued to grin in that unruffled, kindly way he had. "But if the man wishes to leave, there is no way we can stop him, my dear."

"Perhaps not, but if he does choose to leave, I am to be informed of that decision at once. He must not leave before I have had an opportunity to speak with him."

"Very well, if that is what you wish, Vanessa," Simon said. "I'll send word to you as soon as the man is conscious and able to speak."

Seemingly satisfied, Vanessa turned to go.

"Before you leave, Vanessa," Simon said, placing a hand on her arm. "I would very much like to talk to you."

"If you wish to talk about the Mallory lands, I tell you frankly, my father did a foolish thing in turning over the lands to you," she said. "He has asked me not to interfere with that bequest and I will honor his asking...for the moment."

Again Simon and Doc Smithers exchanged knowing glances.

"Your father has asked you to not interfere?" Doc Smithers said, rubbing his chin and eying Vanessa suspiciously.

"Oh, I'm aware that you all believe my father and mother to be dead." She gave her head a toss and laughed. "Well, they're not. They're very much alive. I don't know what the game is that they are playing, but I promised Father not to interfere, and I will not interfere, not at present. But don't think for a moment that I intend to keep that promise. I will get back every acre of

Mallory land. It is mine and I intend to have it."

"But I did not wish to speak to you on that score," Simon said, seemingly unperturbed by her outburst. "It's the new factory which I wanted to talk with you about."

"New factory? What new factory?"

"I thought Brian mentioned it to you last evening."

"I don't care a bit about any new factory."

"But if you care about Bloodstone and your family and yourself," Simon argued, "then you will be most interested to hear about the factory that will eventually destroy all of that."

Vanessa eyed him warily. She didn't want to talk about any factory now. She had to find Tutrice and tell her about the man with the bloodstone.

"Nothing will destroy Bloodstone."

"You must listen to me, Vanessa. It is of the utmost importance."

"I will listen when I am ready to listen," Vanessa said evenly. She turned on her heels and stormed out of the room.

Doc Smithers and Simon Caldwell just stood there listening to the echo of the slammed door. Doc Smithers scratched his chin again and cocked an eye at Simon.

"Crazy as a loon," Simon said.

"Crazy as a loon," Doc Smithers agreed.

CHAPTER ELEVEN

Vanessa saw Brian waiting for her in front of Wilkin's general store.

She didn't have time to talk to Brian now. She skirted the edge of a building and ducked into an alleyway that she knew would take her to a back road that led eventually to Bloodstone. The route was a little longer, but to stand talking, arguing with Brian, would take longer still.

Once she reached the back road, she hoisted her skirts and ran out of Skull Point toward home.

She'd heard the mutterings behind her back. Brian had not wasted any time in spreading the news that Vanessa Mallory was mentally disturbed. Of course it was her own fault but she did not care. Tutrice would think of some way of getting the man to Bloodstone. He had to be the right one this time. He had to be.

"Tutrice," she called excitedly as she came into the house. Tutrice was just coming down the winding staircase. "He's back, Tutrice."

"Who is back, child?"

"The bloodstone. The man with the bloodstone."

Tutrice gave a little gasp, then hurried down the stairs and gripped Vanessa's arm. "What are you saying?"

"He's back, I tell you. I saw him. I found him washed up on the beach." She tried to catch her breath. "They're taking him to Simon Caldwell's. He's still alive. Doctor Smithers said he will be all right."

"Calm yourself, Vanessa. You're making no sense. Come, sit down and tell me calmly."

She led Vanessa into the sitting room. "Now," Tutrice said, seating herself next to Vanessa on the velvet divan. "Tell me what you found. Tell me slowly."

"Well, I was walking toward Skull Point...along the beach... when I stumbled on a man, lying at the edge of the surf. At first I didn't know what to do, but Noah Bingham and some men came along and carried him to Noah's house. One of the men went to fetch Doctor Smithers. The man had obviously been washed overboard from some ship, or his ship broke up in the storm, that's what Noah thinks, but they never saw any wreckage. Anyway, Ruth Bingham began making a fuss about having to keep the man in their home. When Doctor Smithers arrived, he suggested taking the man to Skull Point where he'd be able to look after him."

"But what about the bloodstone?" Tutrice said impatiently.

"While the man was at the Bingham house, we were called into the bedroom because one of the men said the man was coming round. They'd undressed him. Doctor Smithers turned back the coverlet to examine the body and I saw the bloodstone ring, attached by a leather cord around the stranger's neck and lying on his chest."

Tutrice was staring at her. She took a sharp intake of breath. "The bloodstone ring?" she gasped.

"Yes, it was the same ring, I swear it."

"He was wearing it about his neck?"

Vanessa nodded. "It wasn't the same man, Tutrice. This man is younger and of slighter stature. The ring would have fallen off his hand had he been wearing it."

Tutrice stared ahead at nothing. Vanessa frowned. "What is it?" she asked, placing her hand on Tutrice's.

The old woman pulled herself together. "I must apologize to you, dear Vanessa. You were right to follow your intuition. I should have known better. You came back to Bloodstone and you have found him. I was a foolish old woman to try to keep you from returning here."

"Why did you?"

Tutrice made a helpless little gesture. "I thought we could both escape our obligations. I know now that it would have been impossible. The forces that surround us are much too powerful to resist. I should not have tried defying them. But all is well now. I have been made to face reality and we have found the man with the bloodstone ring."

"Oh, Tutrice," Vanessa said with impatience. "Why must you always talk to me in riddles. What forces? What obligations? What reality?"

"I have known for a long time that you belonged here and I tried to keep you away for my own selfish reasons. I was wrong. You are who you are and nothing, not even I, can change that." Suddenly she roused herself and stood up. "We must bring the man here," she said. "Where is the stranger now?"

"Simon Caldwell volunteered to lodge him in his house. He says he has the room and the necessary help to provide. I insisted that the man be brought here to Bloodstone, but Doctor Smithers was most insistent that it would not be proper. They're afraid if they break the stipulation, that no one from town set foot in Bloodstone, there might be legal grounds to take the Mallory lands away from them. He was most insistent that the man be kept out of Bloodstone."

"Then we must get him here of the man's own free will. You will have to do it, Vanessa. You are beautiful. No man will be able to resist your beauty. It will be easy to make him fall in love with you. Once that has been accomplished, everything else will fall into place and the riddles will all come to an end." A look of sadness came over her face and she sighed. "Justice will fall with bloodstone bright. I would have preferred it otherwise, but I know now that I cannot go against that which is ordained."

"That is the part of the riddle I don't understand," Vanessa said, reaching out and taking Tutrice's hand. "Explain it to me."

"That I cannot do, not yet, child. Once the man with the bloodstone is back in this house, it will all be made clear."

"Back? You said 'back' in this house."

"Until the stone is returned, the riddle must remain a riddle. Come, child. We have no time to lose. You must go to Simon Caldwell. Offer your services to nurse the man back to health. Be sure you are the first face he sees when he regains consciousness."

"But Simon doesn't need my services. He has servants enough for two households."

"You must make him want your services. Think of something, anything...but you must be in that house. The man must not escape Skull Point and the prophecy."

"I told Doctor Smithers that I insisted the man not be allowed to leave the village without first advising me."

"I don't trust Doctor Smithers or any of that lot. We cannot rely on anyone but ourselves. Hurry, make yourself as pretty as possible. I will arrange for Carl to hitch the rig. Get back to Skull Point. Get into Simon Caldwell's house on any ruse you can. It should not be difficult. He said he wished to converse with you. Use that as an excuse."

"He wanted to discuss some ridiculous factory."

"A factory?"

"Yes. They are to make munitions in the event of a war with the South."

"Then speak to him of his factory. Do anything you can to endear yourself to him, but do not forget that you are there for one purpose and one purpose only—to get that man with the bloodstone into this house."

"And what then?"

"Then...." Tutrice smiled. "Then everything will be made right and we will be able to put things into their proper places. Your father and mother will explain why they did what they did. I will be able to find peace of mind. You will find happiness. Things will be as they should be. Dreams will come true. Murder will be avenged."

"Murder!"

Tutrice nodded solemnly. "Murder," she repeated.

"I knew nothing of a murder," Vanessa said, startled.

"There was a murder committed in Bloodstone. Many years ago someone died because of another man's greed. The victim's name I cannot divulge. The murderer's name will be divulged when the bloodstone is fitted into its proper place. Then the key will be able to turn the lock and all will be righted." Tutrice was staring off into space. Suddenly she turned and pulled Vanessa to her feet. "But first things first. Off with you, child. I will get Carl. You make yourself lovely. We have no time to lose."

The buggy was hitched under the portico when Vanessa came out a short time later. Carl was holding the reins. At sight of him Vanessa fell back. She wanted nothing to do with the man. He upset her merely by his presence.

"No, Carl. I've changed my mind. It's too lovely a day to ride. I'd prefer to walk into Skull Point." She didn't wait for him to say anything. She turned quickly and went down the drive, She knew he was watching her, and smiling that strange smile.

Simon Caldwell's house sat at the edge of town, the largest and most beautiful house in Skull Point. The wide, spacious drive that led to it had been swept clean. The white paint sparkled, the blue shutters damaged in the storm had been repaired.

Vanessa raised the huge, bronze knocker. A moment later a young girl in a starched white uniform answered her knock.

"I would like to see Mr. Caldwell," she told the servant girl. "I'm Vanessa Mallory."

"Yes, indeed, Miss Mallory. This way please," the girl said, "Mr. Caldwell is expecting you, I believe."

She led Vanessa through a large, airy foyer into a cheerful sitting room of velvet and gold. Like the outside, the interior was handsome and impressive. Simon was sitting before an empty fireplace with a book on his lap. When Vanessa was announced he rose and smiled, extending his hand.

"Vanessa, my dear. I had not hoped to see you so soon." She did not bother to extend her hand. Simon dropped his. "Sit down, Vanessa. Sit down."

"I thought perhaps I might speak with the man you are caring for," she told him.

"Yes, of course," Simon said. "But I am afraid he has not come around fully as yet. He is still sleeping. Doctor Smithers left just a short while ago. He should be returning before long, however."

"I did not come to speak with Doctor Smithers .I believe I've said all I intend to say to him."

"Well, let me serve you some tea," Simon said. "I was hoping to have a little chat with you."

"I do not wish to discuss anything but the man in your upstairs bedroom."

Simon chose to ignore her remark. "You are looking exceeding well, Vanessa. I heard you had not been well. It grieved me to hear it, but I am very pleased to see you are up and around as usual."

"You saw me earlier, Simon. I haven't changed in so short a time."

"I saw you when you were slightly distressed, my dear. I trust you have calmed yourself."

"I am quite calm and I am quite determined to speak with the man I found on the beach."

"You know him then?"

"Yes," Vanessa lied. "I do."

"But why did you not say earlier that you knew his name?"

"I did not say I knew his name. I just said I know him," Vanessa said icily.

Simon gave her a quizzical look. She gave him a frosty stare and said, "I am not as mentally unbalanced as people say."

"But how can you know a man and not know his name?"

"We met but were not introduced."

"Where did you meet?" Simon asked.

To Vanessa's relief there was a flurry of skirts and scuffling footsteps. A short, stout woman came into the room. "Pardon, Mr. Caldwell, but the young man is waking up, sir," she said hurriedly. "He's opened his eyes."

Simon and Vanessa were on their feet in an instant. Simon

led the way with Vanessa close on his heels. They went up the stairs quickly. Simon opened a door and Vanessa pushed herself past him. The handsome young man from the sea lay on the bed, staring up at the ceiling. When they entered the room he turned his head. His eyes rested first on Vanessa. He smiled at her.

"Hello," he said in a lilting voice. "And who might you be, lovely lady?"

But Vanessa didn't hear him. The coverlet was pulled back. She was staring at his naked chest.

"The bloodstone," she gasped. "It's gone."

CHAPTER TWELVE

She was the most beautiful thing in the world...if he was in the world. The man in the bed wondered if he was dead, or surely dreaming.

"Where is it?" Vanessa asked. "What happened to the bloodstone?"

"What bloodstone?" Simon asked, looking at her with astonishment. "What are you talking about?" Inside his head he heard Doctor Smithers say, "Crazy as a loon."

But Vanessa was staring at the man in the bed. She did not see his handsome face now. She only saw the naked chest where the bloodstone ring had rested.

He eased the coverlet up under his chin and felt across his chest. "I guess I lost it in the sea," he said. He didn't seem concerned.

"No. You had it when I found you. It was around your neck. Someone has stolen it."

Simon was trying to understand. "What are you raving about, child? Who has stolen what?"

Vanessa turned on him. "He was wearing the bloodstone on a chain about his neck. It is gone."

The man in the bed didn't take his eyes off Vanessa. He did not care about the bloodstone. He felt glad to be rid of it at last. This wouldn't be the first time it had been taken. There had been too many thefts and he felt suddenly relieved that he'd have to guard it no more. He should have thrown it into the sea long ago, but something always held him back.

"You took it," she said. "Where is it, Simon? What have you done with it?"

"Calm yourself, Vanessa," he said, "The man had nothing around his neck when he was brought here. I saw no bloodstone."

"You did. You took it. Who else could have stolen it?"

"Well," Simon said slowly, rationally, "if you say he was wearing a gem around his neck when you found the man, then any one of a number of people could have removed it. The man was unconscious for a while at the Binghams and several of the townspeople following the litter might have taken it. He was not wearing any such stone when he was carried into this house."

"You're lying."

"Now why would I lie? I have no need for a bloodstone. One Bloodstone in Skull Point is quite sufficient."

The man in the bed stirred. "If I may be so bold as to interrupt," he said. "If you two can forget my bloodstone for a moment, I would very much like to know precisely where I am."

"You're in my home. I am Simon Caldwell. This is the town of Skull Point in New England."

The man gave him a blank look. "Skull Point? I'm afraid I have never heard of it."

"We're a small fishing village. And now that I have answered your question, perhaps you will tell us who you are and how you happened to get yourself washed up on our shore."

"My name's Malcolm Drew. There was a storm. I was swept off the deck of my ship."

"And what ship might that be?" Simon asked.

"The *Sea Serpent,* bound for Boston harbor."

"Out of where?"

"What do you care where or what or who? What happened to the bloodstone?" Vanessa insisted.

Malcolm Drew smiled at her. "Don't bother your pretty head about the ring, miss. It will find its way back to me. It always has in the past."

"What do you mean?"

"Just that. The stone has been lost and stolen many times before. I've always recovered it, even though I never search for it. Frankly, I'm just as pleased to be rid of the thing."

"You mustn't say that."

"Why is the stone so important to you, miss?"

Vanessa faltered. "I don't know. It just is."

Simon interrupted them. "Mr. Drew, this young lady is Vanessa Mallory. She claims you and she have met before, although you were not introduced."

"That is not entirely true," she said, a little shamefacedly. "It was the ring that I'd seen before."

Simon grinned, pleased with himself for knowing that she'd lied earlier. "Miss Mallory lives in the estate on the bluff. The place is called Bloodstone. Perhaps she feels some sort of affinity toward anything bearing that name."

"It isn't exactly that," she said. "I must find...." She didn't finish the sentence. How could she explain? She couldn't.

"Yes, Mr. Caldwell is right," she said, forcing a smile. "I do have an affinity for anything connected with Bloodstone. The ring you carried was very beautiful. I was disappointed at seeing it gone, is all. Tell us about yourself, Mr. Drew. Where is your ship now? Were you its captain?"

"I don't know where the ship might be at present. And yes, I was its captain."

Simon frowned. "You look much too young to be a sea captain."

"Looks are sometimes deceiving," Malcolm said.

"And where do you come from, captain?" Vanessa asked.

"The sea is my home, Miss Vanessa. I have no land roots."

Again the words in the Bible flashed before her eyes. "Bloodstone, bloodstone out of the sea." She found herself saying them aloud.

Simon gave her a strange look. Crazy as a loon, he thought. "We should let Mr. Drew rest, Vanessa. Are you hungry, young man? I'll have one of the maids fix you something."

"No, thank you, sir. I'm afraid my stomach is too filled with salt water to crave food."

"Then rest yourself, lad. If you want anything there's a bell pull just at the head of the bed."

Simon turned to go. He stood, waiting for Vanessa to join him.

Vanessa smiled at Malcolm. "If you are not overly tired, Mr. Drew, perhaps you would like me to sit and visit with you for a while."

"I'd like that very much," Malcolm said, returning her brilliant smile.

Simon started to object. Vanessa pulled a chair closer to the bed and without looking at Simon, said, "Leave the door open, Simon, if you are worried about propriety."

Simon went, hesitantly, leaving the door wide open.

"So you live in a house called Bloodstone?" Malcolm said as Vanessa adjusted her skirts around her.

"Yes. It's on the bluff overlooking the sea."

Malcolm's brows knit together. "Strange," he said, "but I feel I've heard that name before."

"You have. You wore it around your neck."

He chuckled. "No, the house I mean. I feel that it's been mentioned to me before, but I can't think by whom. It was a long, long time ago, I believe."

"Have you always worn the bloodstone ring around your neck?" Vanessa asked.

"Yes, ever since my father presented it to me."

"Your father gave it to you?"

"His hand was large enough to accommodate the ring. I'm afraid my build is not as grand as his."

"Your build, if I may use that word, is most becoming, sir," Vanessa said boldly.

"I doubt if Mr. Caldwell would approve of a young lady making so bold a remark."

"Pooh on Mr. Caldwell. I do and say what I wish."

Malcolm found he could not stop looking at her. "Do you live at Bloodstone with your husband?"

It was Vanessa's turn to laugh. "Husband? Mercy no. I have no husband."

He felt wonderfully relieved. Happiness was one luxury he'd never allowed himself. But now he was happy.

"I live with my parents and my guardian, Tutrice."

"Tutrice? What a strange name."

"It means 'guardian.'"

"Odd, but I feel I've heard that name before also."

"It's not a name one forgets easily."

In spite of the happiness he felt, the mention of the old guardian's name put a weight around his heart.

"Here, let me fluff your pillows," Vanessa said. She stood and leaned over the bed. Malcolm raised himself up. Their faces were mere inches apart. He looked deep into her eyes. "You are very beautiful," he murmured.

Vanessa smiled and felt the color rising in her cheeks. A tremor ran through her body as she fluffed the pillows and then innocently rested her hand against his cheek. "Thank you, Malcolm Drew," she said.

He could not control himself. The touch of her hand set him on fire. He seized her hand and pressed it to his lips.

Vanessa felt the hot flames flash through her. She closed her eyes as the room began to spin around.

Suddenly she regained her senses. Her face was flushed crimson. She pulled her hand away from his mouth, turned and ran blindly from the room, leaving Malcolm sitting in the bed staring after her.

"Tomorrow," she heard him call. She rushed down the stairs, ignoring Simon Caldwell, who stood at the bottom, and ran out of the house.

"Vanessa," Brian called as she raced past him. "Vanessa, stop, please. I must speak with you."

He hurried after her, catching her by one arm. She was out of breath. There were tears in her eyes.

"What is it? What's wrong, Vanessa?" Brian asked when he saw her agitated condition. He shook her gently. "Tell me, my dearest, what has upset you so?"

She managed to open her eyes and focus on him. "It's nothing," she managed to say. "Nothing at all."

"No, something has upset you. Tell me."

Vanessa couldn't think. She felt Brian shake her again. She reopened her eyes and looked at him. The contrast between the two men was shocking, so shocking that Vanessa came immediately to her senses.

"What has happened? Where were you racing off to?"

"Bloodstone," Vanessa managed to say. She shrugged herself free of his grip. "I must get home. The stone. It's gone. Someone has stolen it."

"The stone? What stone? What are you talking about?"

"The bloodstone around Malcolm's neck. Someone has stolen it."

"Please, Vanessa. Calm yourself. You're making no sense."

Suddenly Vanessa wanted to be rid of Brian. "Go away, Brian. Let me be."

She had to find Tutrice and tell her about the stolen ring. They had to retrieve it and return it to Malcolm. Then she could love him; they could be married; they'd live in Bloodstone forever and the mystery of the Bible would be solved.

She had no time for Brian now. She turned on her heels and started away from him.

"Wait," he called. "Tell me what this is all about. Vanessa." He caught up with her.

"It has nothing to do with you, Brian. Forgive me for being rude but I haven't time to stand and talk with you. I've something very important to attend to."

"What? Tell me."

"The man I found on the beach was wearing a huge bloodstone ring on a chain about his neck. When I visited him at Simon's, the bloodstone ring was missing. Someone took it."

"Oh, Vanessa. Who in Skull Point would do such a thing? The ring most likely came loose and fell off somewhere while they were carrying him here to town. Perhaps Noah Bingham knows where it is." He paused and looked at her as they hurried along. "But why is the man's ring so important?"

"It's a bloodstone ring. The Mallory house is called Bloodstone. There's a connection. I can't explain it, Brian. I don't know myself what significance Malcolm's ring has, but I know it is extremely important."

"Malcolm?"

Vanessa flushed. "The man I found on the beach. His name is Malcolm Drew."

"You called him Malcolm. Isn't that rather familiar, Vanessa?"

"Don't be so stodgy, Brian. You're worse than Simon Caldwell. I can say it if I want. Malcolm, Malcolm, Malcolm... there!" She suddenly slowed her steps and looked back toward Simon Caldwell's house.

A cold shiver went through Brian. He didn't know her any more. He reached out and put his hand on her arm.

Vanessa stiffened and pulled her arm away. "Don't touch me, Brian. Don't ever touch me. No one will ever touch me except him," she said. She turned and again ran as fast as she could in the direction of Bloodstone. She'd found him. The words of the poem filled her thoughts; "Bloodstone, bloodstone out of the sea...only with that can true love be."

CHAPTER THIRTEEN

Malcolm Drew sat in bed staring at the door through which Vanessa had vanished. Simon Caldwell appeared in it. He nodded. "I must apologize for Miss Mallory. She is a rather strange young woman, Mr. Drew."

"But the most beautiful woman I have ever seen."

"Yes, I cannot deny that." Simon hesitated, as if choosing his words carefully. "She seemed unduly concerned about your lost bloodstone. I wonder why?"

"She is a fiery woman, I must say."

Simon looked grim. "She is not well, I'm sorry to say. She had an accident, a blow to the head, I'm told. She isn't...er... herself."

Malcolm frowned at him. "You mean she is mentally unbalanced?"

"Well, not totally unbalanced. She just acts a bit peculiarly at times. I would be very careful not to become involved with her. She is sometimes not responsible for what she says and does. She's been away from Skull Point for many years and has only recently returned. She found her parents had died during her absence. She refuses to accept that fact and insists that they are still alive and living in the family manor house, Bloodstone." His eyes brightened. "I suppose that is why she puts importance upon your bloodstone. Perhaps she feels it akin to her home."

"Possibly," Malcolm said. But his thoughts were not on the bloodstone. His thoughts were on Vanessa.

"You say you were headed for Boston harbor, Captain

Drew?" Simon said interrupting Malcolm's thoughts. "Where do you hail from?"

"As I said earlier, the sea is my home. However, I was born in Norfolk."

"That's in Virginia, is it not?"

"Yes."

"Then you are a Southerner. But you have no trace of Southern accent."

"It comes out at times. I went to sea very young. With all the ports of call I've visited, I suppose I left a bit of my Southern drawl in each one of them."

"But what are you doing so far north?"

"Oh, I didn't sail out of Virginia this time. We were coming down from Newfoundland when we encountered the storm."

"Then I take it you are not involved in the political struggle presently going on between the North and the South?"

"I'm a sailor, not a politician, Mr. Caldwell."

"But if there is a civil war, which seems inevitable, you will be expected to choose sides?"

"I will try to remain neutral if at all possible. As I said, my home is the sea, nowhere else. I have no geographical roots except the water. Whichever ocean I am on, that is my home."

"And you intend to return to it?"

"Of course. There is no other place for me."

Simon seated himself in the chair Vanessa had vacated. "I can understand your love for the sea," Simon said. "Although I have never lived on it, I could never live far from it. There is something mysterious and beautiful about it, I must agree."

"Mysterious and beautiful and very comforting." He sighed. "Already I long to get back to it."

"Not for a few days, my boy. Doctor Smithers says you must rest." He reached out and patted Malcolm's shoulder. "Stay in Skull Point. It is a quiet little town, but most charming. I believe you will enjoy it."

"Skull Point. What an ominous name for such a quaint little village."

"It was once a pirates' lair. It is said it was used as a graveyard for the plunderers' victims. That's how it got its name."

"Buried treasure too?" Malcolm said, amused.

Simon laughed. "No, I'm afraid there is no treasure here. The only jewel here is Bloodstone, the Mallory mansion, if one can call that broken-down old relic a jewel."

"Of course there is Vanessa Mallory herself. She is indeed a jewel."

Simon smiled and nodded again. "But speaking of jewels, you do not seem too anxious about the bloodstone Miss Mallory said was around your neck."

"I'm not. It will come back to me. It always has."

"I don't understand."

Malcolm shook his head. "I don't either, really. The ring was always in our family, I'm told. It has been lost and stolen many times over the years but has always been returned to the owner. For instance, about five or six years ago I met a sea captain in Calcutta, a huge hulk of a man, as big as a house almost. He admired the bloodstone and asked if he could purchase it from me. Although his price was most attractive and I was in need of money, I found I could not sell the stone.

"That night the ring disappeared, as did the sea captain. Then just a few years ago I met the man again. He was far from the same man I'd known. He'd shrunk in size. He looked sick, almost to the point of death. He cursed me and threw the ring back at me, saying it was evil, that a devil lived inside the stone."

Simon was leaning forward with intent interest.

"And he was not the first man to take the bloodstone, then search me out so that he could return it to me. Always they said the same thing, that there was a devil living inside the stone."

"But surely that is just plain nonsense. There are no such things as evil spirits," Simon said.

Malcolm shrugged his shoulders. "Who's to say?"

Simon's housekeeper tapped on the open door. "Excuse me, Mr. Caldwell, but Brian McGrath is downstairs and wishes a word with you."

"Send him up here, Louisa." He turned to Malcolm. "You don't mind, do you, Captain Drew?"

"Not at all."

A moment later Brian entered the room. Simon made the introductions and then said, "What is it you want with me, Brian? I trust it isn't anything that cannot be discussed in Captain Drew's presence."

Brian gave them both a nervous glance. "It's about Vanessa, Simon. She seemed more irrational than ever when I ran into her coming away from your house. I was wondering if you could enlighten me as to what has upset her so."

"Vanessa?" Malcolm said. "You refer to Miss Mallory?"

"Yes, my fiancée," Brian said.

"Your fiancée?" Malcolm's face darkened. "Surely she does not intend to marry *you*?"

Brian gave him a frosty look. "She has not openly proclaimed our engagement but it is understood that we will marry one day."

Malcolm laughed. "Oh, I see. In other words, you consider yourself engaged; she does not."

"Sir," Brian said icily, "Vanessa and I will marry. Everyone knows it."

"Everyone perhaps but Miss Mallory."

"Contain yourselves, gentlemen," Simon said.

"She is not a well girl," Brian snapped. "If you have upset her in any way, Captain, you will have me to answer to."

Malcolm laughed in his face. "You have no claim on the girl. If you intend to marry her, be prepared to fight for her."

"Gentlemen, gentlemen," Simon put in. "You are both behaving rather brashly. Come along, Brian. Let us leave Captain Drew to his rest. You and I can discuss whatever is bothering you down in my study. Come along." He took Brian's arm. Brian let himself be pulled from the room.

Brian was beside himself with temper by the time they reached Simon's study. "Here, have some sherry," Simon said. "It will help calm you down."

Brian waved it away. He paced for a while in an effort to

bring himself under control. "How dare he insinuate...."

"He insinuated nothing, Brian. He's just a young lad who met an attractive woman. He is brash and headstrong. He is from the sea and therefore his behavior is quite different from our own. Pay him no mind. He will be gone in a few days and will forget all about Vanessa."

"Then I am right in assuming he was responsible for Vanessa's distraught state of mind?"

Simon shrugged. "I admit there seemed an immediate attraction. I was not in the room when she became upset. Knowing sailors, I would venture to guess that Captain Drew allowed himself to be forward with her."

"I'll thrash the man," Brian shouted, starting for the door.

Simon grabbed him. "There will be no quarreling under my roof. Behave yourself, Brian. You are as hot-headed as the lad upstairs. Sit down. Have some sherry."

"No," Brian said angrily. But he did sit.

"Vanessa is the least of our worries," Simon said. "We must do something to stop the construction of that factory. It has got to be built somewhere other than here in Skull Point. I understand the contractors will be here in a few days to begin their ground-breaking. I've tried mentioning the factory to Vanessa but she is not at all interested, as you told me."

"No, she's not interested."

"We must make her interested. That factory has got to be located somewhere else—not here in Skull Point. It will be the end of us all."

"But there are people in Skull Point who want the factory." Brian said.

"They must not be able to rally Vanessa to their side of the argument. We both know that the Mallory name throws a lot of weight in certain important political circles. Her father was a personal friend of the governor's."

Brian ran his hands through his hair. "But if Vanessa isn't interested, she isn't interested. You know how difficult she can be once she has made up her mind to something."

"She will become interested if we go about her the right way."

"What do you mean?"

Simon's mind was working fast. "Vanessa has an unnatural concern for a certain bloodstone ring which Captain Drew was wearing around his neck. That ring has mysteriously disappeared. Why Vanessa wants the ring, I don't know, but if we were to find the bloodstone we might persuade her to do as we ask."

"I see," Brian said; but he did not see. "This bloodstone ring, do you know where it is?"

"I have a very good idea," Simon said. "I'm not absolutely positive, but I have a feeling I know its whereabouts."

"You say the bloodstone ring belongs to that man upstairs?"

"Yes, he said he wears it about his neck. He thinks it was lost at sea when he floundered in the water. Vanessa says she saw it around his neck when she found him on the beach. The man does not seem overly concerned about the ring. He claims there is a sort of curse on it and that it always finds its way back to him whenever it becomes lost or stolen. Naturally I do not believe in nonsense such as that. My only concern about the bloodstone is that Vanessa wants the bloodstone for her own personal reasons. We will get it for her, but in return she will have to intercede for us with the governor and see that the factory is not built here in Skull Point."

"Noah Bingham and his crowd won't agree with you. They say they want the factory. It would give them a market for their catches. Zeb Brewster and Jonah Black would make more money on their farm products."

"What farm products? They have not produced enough to feed themselves, let alone sell any products to the public. But be that as it may, the important thing is that the factory must not be built here."

"But you control the lands hereabouts. All you have to do is simply not sell any land to the contractors."

"That is the problem. Jeremiah, I believe, has already given over land to them. There are certain deeds to lands which were not given over to me—I mean to the town—when he died."

"Then we must get those deeds back."

"That is precisely what I am saying. Only Vanessa can help us do that. And I think she will."

"She will want all the deeds returned to her."

"No doubt she will. She so much as told me so. But I will have to worry about that after the factory problem is settled."

"She has no legal claim to the lands, does she?"

"She might. Remember, Jeremiah and Hester believed she was dead when they made out their wills. A court of law may reverse the conditions of the wills now that they know Vanessa Mallory is alive and has returned. Of course if Vanessa weren't alive...."

"Simon! What are you thinking?"

Simon laughed. "No, no, of course I could never do anything to harm the poor child. I was merely dreaming. I'm as fond of her as you are, Brian, my boy. If she had drowned, however, then all of these problems would cease to exist." He sighed.

"The factory would still be a problem."

"True. True."

"Of course if Vanessa and I married, then I would be able to act on her behalf, would I not?" Brian said.

Simon laughed. "Act on Vanessa's behalf? I doubt it very much, knowing our dear Vanessa." He chuckled again. "You'd be lucky to act on your own behalf, my boy."

Brian lowered his head. "I feel guilty, as though I were plotting against her. I truly love her, Simon. I want nothing else in the world but to be married to her and to make her my wife."

"Very admirable, my boy. Very admirable. And one day it will all be the way you want it. There is no one else in Skull Point worthy of a girl like Vanessa Mallory."

"But she might run away again as she did once before."

"She might." His eyes happened to look upward, toward the upstairs bedroom. "I don't think she'd run very far with Captain Drew, however."

"First things first, Brian. We must find the bloodstone ring.

We must not return it to Captain Drew—not until Vanessa has agreed to do what we wish. The ring is the most important thing at the moment."

"You say you know where it is?"

"I have a very good idea," Simon told him. "Come. Let us go and see if I am right."

CHAPTER FOURTEEN

For the third time in one day Vanessa found herself on foot making the trip back to the village.

Tutrice had been no help. Vanessa was annoyed with her as she started out to begin her search for the lost bloodstone. She decided that the Bingham house would be the most logical place to begin. That was where she had seen the ring.

Vanessa really wanted to go to Simon Caldwell's. Malcolm Drew was there. But, Noah's first.

It was on the near side of midnight and the moon had taken refuge behind some far-flung clouds. The stars were dimmed by a thick veil, although here and there one broke through and twinkled and blinked. Vanessa had wrapped herself in a heavy, warm cloak to keep out the chill of the night. A cool wind blew in from the sea, flapping at her skirts and stinging her cheeks. She hugged the cloak around her as she went toward Noah Bingham's house.

She was relieved to see that a light burned in Noah's window. She was glad she would not have to rouse them from their beds. She had thought of waiting until morning, but Tutrice had said time was of the essence and by morning the bloodstone ring might well find its way out of Skull Point.

As Vanessa got nearer the house she saw the light in the window vanish, and a dimmer light bloomed behind the thick curtains of the bedroom window. She went like a ghost along the walk to the front door and tapped lightly. She heard the murmur of voices, low and indistinct, then the shuffling of feet.

Noah Bingham cracked open the door.

"Miss Vanessa," he said when he recognized her, swinging the door open wide. "You gave us a start. What brings you here at so late a time of night?"

"I must speak with you, Noah. May I come in?"

"Of course, child."

"Who is it?" Ruth called, hurrying out of the bedroom, wrapping her night coat around her ample frame. When she saw Vanessa she crossed her arms across her bosom. "Lord, Miss Vanessa, we thought it was a night specter come to call."

"I realize it is very late," Vanessa said, "but my business could not wait until morning. I've come about the bloodstone ring Malcolm Drew was wearing when he was carried here from the beach."

Noah and Ruth exchanged looks. "How strange," Noah said. "Simon Caldwell was here earlier this evening with Brian. They told us the man's name and asked about the same ring."

Vanessa's expression darkened. "So," she said, breathing the word through clenched teeth. "I should have known."

"Known what, dear?" Ruth asked.

Vanessa shook her head impatiently. "It's nothing." She tried to think. "Did you give him the bloodstone?"

"We know nothing of a bloodstone ring," Noah said. "I admit I saw the ring around the young man's neck, but it was there when they carried him into the town."

"You're sure of that?"

Ruth pushed herself forward. "We wouldn't be lying to you," she said, showing a glimmer of temper.

"No, of course you wouldn't," Vanessa said. "I just thought...." She did not know really what she thought. She looked at Noah imploringly. "It is very important that I find that ring."

"But surely the ring does not belong to you," Ruth said.

"In a way, it does," Vanessa said. "I think it was taken from Bloodstone a long, long time ago. It is necessary that it be returned."

"Taken from Bloodstone. Surely that young man is no thief,"

Noah said.

Vanessa shook her head. "No, it wasn't his doing. The ring was taken long before his or our time. Please, Noah. I can't explain. It is all very confusing. I don't understand it myself. All I know is that I must find the bloodstone ring and return it to Bloodstone Manor. I wish I could tell you why but I don't know myself."

Again Noah and Ruth exchanged looks and Vanessa read them easily. They were remembering what Brian McGrath had said about her mental state. She was suddenly sorry she'd played that little game with Brian. Things were getting out of hand.

"I'm not insane," she said out of the blue. "I know what is being said about me, but it just isn't true. I realize I've been acting strangely since I returned, but...." She cut herself off. She realized she was making no sense.

"The bloodstone ring is not here then," she said instead.

"We know nothing of a bloodstone ring," Ruth said emphatically.

"And you didn't give it to Simon Caldwell?"

"Really," Ruth said, her temper showing. "I do believe you've intruded on us long enough. We told you we didn't give it to Simon. We haven't seen the ring since it left this house around the neck of the man who owns it."

"Now, Ruth," Noah said. "Calm yourself. Miss Vanessa is obviously upset."

Vanessa shook her head. "I must get to Simon's. I must find the bloodstone ring tonight."

"Can't it wait until morning, child? It's very late, you know."

"No, I can't wait until morning." She turned and pulled open the door and ran out into the night.

She ran along the road the men had taken when they carried Malcolm's litter into Skull Point. But there was a shorter route, she decided, looking at the little zigzag path that went off to the right. A mist was beginning to settle as she stepped onto the path and went quickly between the trees and black-green bushes that short-circuited the sweeping curve of the main road. The path was wide and clear, making her going easy. Occasionally the path crossed little ribbons of water, but either stepping stones or crude little bridges removed any obstacle the creeks might present.

As she rounded a sharp turn her foot tangled in a tree root and she fell face forward. As she fell something struck the trunk of the tree beside her, sounding like a hand slapping the bark. A fraction of a second later she heard a sharp crack, the crack of a rifle.

Someone had shot at her. Out there in the darkness stood a marksman who had tried to murder her. Would he think he had succeeded? Would he go away if she stayed motionless on the ground? She was afraid to move.

Murder. Tutrice had spoken of murder. But whose murder? It was all connected to the bloodstone ring.

She raised her head and looked back along the path she had taken. The path ran between widely spaced trees and shrubs. She scanned the slopes of open wood above her. The wood seemed apparently empty. She saw no movement, heard no sound. Whoever was hunting her with rifle in hand had obviously thought he'd hit his mark and left her for dead.

He? Vanessa wondered. Perhaps it was not a man at all.

Slowly she got to her feet, and hurried along the edge of the path, moving as quickly and as cautiously as she dared. The path twisted and turned for several yards. Then directly ahead she saw the road and the first building that started the town proper. She ran, keeping to the shelter of trees and brush.

She reached the road, hesitated, made sure no one was lurking with a loaded rifle. She suddenly heard voices and saw three men coming along the road, laughing and talking among themselves. She recognized Josh Lancey—the man who'd helped Noah carry Malcolm up from the beach.

"Josh," she called and ran toward him.

The three men stopped and stood staring at her. "Miss Mallory," Josh said, as she ran up to him. "What on earth...?"

"Someone just shot at me," Vanessa said breathlessly. "I must get to Simon Caldwell's. Will you take me there, please?"

The three men looked at one another and then stared back at Vanessa.

"But Simon is surely abed by this time of night, Miss Vanessa."

"Then I will awaken him," Vanessa insisted. "Come with me, please, Josh. I'm afraid."

She knew she sounded mad, but she didn't care. She didn't care about anything except reaching Simon Caldwell and seeing Malcolm Drew again and finding the bloodstone ring.

The three men continued to look at her skeptically. Two of them backed away, leaving Josh standing with her clinging to him. Josh too wanted to back away from her but she seemed so frantic, so frightened he felt obliged to help the girl, regardless of what her mental state might be.

"Of course, Miss Vanessa. Come along. I'll go with you. No one is trying to hurt you."

"They are, they are," Vanessa cried. "But they mustn't...not until I find the bloodstone."

Josh put his arm around her and tried to reassure her that his strength and presence would protect her. He led her down the street past the general store, past Doctor Smithers' house and office. A lamp was burning in Doctor Smithers' window and Doctor Smithers' silhouette could be seen pacing back and forth in front of that lighted lamp.

"You say someone tried to kill you, Miss Vanessa?"

"Yes."

"Of course with you back now, I wouldn't put it past Noah Bingham to try something like that."

"Noah!" Vanessa stood motionless. She stared up at Josh's rough, weather-beaten face.

Josh looked nervous. He realized that he'd spoken without too much thought behind it. He cursed that final mug of ale he'd had at Cal Andrews' place. He shrugged, knowing that as long as he'd said what he did he was obligated to follow through. "Well," he started, "you know, of course, that your father willed your family properties to Skull Point."

"Yes, I know all about that."

"Well, you've come back. Wouldn't it be only natural for you to try to reclaim your property? Simon wouldn't like that much, neither would Noah or the doctor and any number of other people."

"But why? I can see Simon's reason. He's appointed himself king of Skull Point and enjoys the power his position gives him, but what have the others to lose if I reclaim my rightful property?"

"Noah, now, he wants this here munitions factory built." He glanced at her. "You heard about that? Everybody's talking about that factory—Noah, especially. He's sure you'll be against it."

"But what have I to do with the factory?"

"Well, with the land belonging to Skull Point, Noah thinks he can get his people—Zeb Brewster, Jonah Black, and that crowd—to stand up to Simon and the others who are against building the factory."

Vanessa shook her head. "All right, if you say the factory is that important to both Simon and Noah, I believe you. But you mentioned Doctor Smithers. Why on earth would Doctor Smithers have reason to want to see me dead?"

Josh scratched his chin. "I don't think I should be telling you this, Miss Vanessa." He looked down at her and hesitated.

"You've got to tell me, Josh. Please. Please." She gripped his arm.

"Well, old Doc Smithers has his own personal reasons for not liking you back here in Skull Point."

He hesitated again and wet his lips. "They say he killed your pa."

CHAPTER FIFTEEN

"Killed my father? What are you saying? My father isn't dead."

Josh looked away from her. He'd heard about how strange she was since her accident. He shrugged. "I'm only repeating what folks are saying. Doc Smithers was deep in debt to your people. He had no way of paying back the money your old daddy loaned to him. They say he killed him because of it."

"But my father is very much alive."

"Please, Miss Vanessa, don't say anything about my telling you all this. It would put me in a terrible lot of trouble."

Vanessa was beginning to understand. If a threat had been made on her father's life—a threat that had not succeeded—then perhaps that was why her parents wanted everybody to believe the threat had been successful and they were hiding themselves in Bloodstone to prevent future threats.

If that were the case...if everyone suspected her parents of being dead...if Doctor Smithers had tried to murder them...then it was old Doctor Smithers who was trying to kill her now.

But why hadn't her father warned her? Why had he made such a dark secret about the whole incident?

"There's no proof he did 'em in, Miss," Josh said. "It's only gossip. Personally I don't believe any of it. The old doc's always been a decent enough man. Of course, of late, I must admit he has grown pretty fond of his rum bottle."

"Josh. I'm indebted to you." She was suddenly not afraid. She didn't have time to be afraid. She'd go to Simon and hear what he had to say about this munitions factory they all seemed so concerned about. She'd confront Doctor Smithers when it became necessary. She'd confront all of them. How dare they take sides against a Mallory?

"You needn't accompany me any farther, Josh. I can find Simon Caldwell's house from here."

"But it ain't safe, miss. Come along. I'll go the rest of the way with you."

She looked up at him. She couldn't trust anyone, she told herself. Even Brian might be against her. There was no one.

No, she thought suddenly. There was one, however, whom she felt she could trust. The man who had come from the sea. The man with the bloodstone ring. Malcolm Drew. She knew instinctively she could trust him.

She let Josh walk with her to Simon's house. They spoke little on the way. There was a lamp burning in the downstairs study of Simon's house. "Someone's about," Josh said. "I'll leave you here, then. Please say nothing of what I told you. It wouldn't go well for me, you know."

"I appreciate what you've told me, Josh. I'll keep it in the strictest of confidence, you can be assured. Thank you." She held out her hand.

Josh took it and smiled at her. "Well, good night, miss. If I can be of any help you have but to ask."

"Thank you."

She felt very alone standing at the door to Simon Caldwell's handsome house, staring at the light in the window. The hour was very late; she thought it strange that lights were burning in Noah's house and in Simon's house, and she now remembered seeing a light in Doctor Smithers' window. She frowned.

Was the entire world against her?

She lifted the heavy knocker and let it bang down. It took only a moment before the door opened a crack and Simon Caldwell peered out. When he saw her he smiled and opened the door all the way. He was smiling that false way he had of smiling. His eyes said he was surprised to see her, but his voice said otherwise.

"Come in, Vanessa. What brings you out so late at night?" He stepped aside to let her pass. "You've just missed seeing Brian by half an hour."

Vanessa frowned slightly. Half an hour ago someone had taken a shot at her in the woods. Did Brian also have reasons of his own for wanting her dead? She couldn't think of what they might be, but strange things had happened since she'd left Skull Point. Anything was possible, under the present circumstances. Perhaps Brian had been told of her obvious interest in Malcolm Drew. Perhaps Brian was afraid he might lose her and would rather see her dead than in love with another man.

"I've come about the bloodstone, Simon. Noah tells me you too are searching for it."

"Yes, that's true," Simon admitted, motioning toward the study. "Come. Join us in a glass of sherry or a cup of tea, perhaps."

"Us?" Vanessa hesitated.

"Yes, Captain Drew is in the study. We've been talking. He certainly is a hardy lad. He refuses to stay in bed. Says he is fit as a fiddle."

"Miss Mallory, what a wonderful surprise," Malcolm said as she came into the room. He rose from his chair and went to her, taking her hands in his.

The moment she saw his eyes she knew no one had talked against her—or if they did, Malcolm did not believe them. Vanessa found herself smiling.

"Sit down, Vanessa," Simon said. "May I offer you some refreshment?"

"No, nothing, thank you." She spoke to Simon, but her eyes stayed fixed on Malcolm. His gaze brought a blush to her cheeks. She lowered her eyes, but it took an effort.

Simon cleared his throat when he noticed the intense interest the two young people had in one another. "You were at Noah's, you say?"

Vanessa forced herself to look toward Simon. "Yes. I went

about Captain Drew's bloodstone."

"And did you find it?"

"You know I did not," she said, a little sharper than she had intended. "You yourself went there searching for it. Noah told me as much."

Simon fanned out his hands. "I was merely looking for it to help you, my child. It seemed so important to you."

Malcolm leaned into the conversation. "As I said, I wouldn't concern yourselves about my bloodstone ring. It will show up. It always does."

"I can't explain it, Captain Drew, but the ring seems very important to me for some reason or other. It has to do with my family's Bible. I know you will think me quite odd, but there is a strange poem in the Bible that has haunted me since I was a little girl. Our house was named for a large bloodstone. The jewel was stolen from the house centuries ago, or so I believe. A matter of justice rests with the return of the stone. I believe the ring you wore around your neck is the stone for which I search."

Malcolm smiled and encouraged her to continue.

"I found the stone on a man's hand some five years ago. But I lost both the man and the stone."

"Tell me about this man," Malcolm urged.

"He was a sea captain. His name is of no importance," she added, glancing cautiously at Simon. "The stone he wore was the very stone you had around your neck. I'm certain of it."

"That very well could be, Miss Mallory. You see, the stone was taken from me more than five years ago by a sea captain, a man I met in the Orient. He returned it to me, however, under rather strange circumstances."

"Then it is the bloodstone, the one which I must return to my home."

"You are more than welcome to it. I have always disliked the stone. It was part of my inheritance, but I never felt comfortable wearing it." Malcolm moved to stand by the vacant fireplace. "Unfortunately, I no longer have the ring, but when it is returned I shall see that you have it, if that is what you wish."

"More than anything in the world."

Simon's eyes moved from the young couple to a locked cabinet that stood against the wall, a cabinet that contained a bloodstone ring—a ring which Doctor Smithers had taken from around Malcolm Drew's neck.

He had intended to tell Vanessa he'd found the ring, but now—looking at the young couple—something told him the time was not right. He would use the ring as a lure. He would wait until Malcolm Drew left Skull Point, and then he would present Vanessa with the ring on condition that she intercede on his behalf with the governor of the state.

He would have to get Malcolm away at the earliest possible moment. But as he watched Vanessa and Malcolm together he realized that it was going to be difficult to separate them easily and quickly. He would get Brian to help him, even if it took violence.

Simon gave a nervous little cough. "I had intended to speak to you about the construction of a munitions factory proposed for location here in Skull Point, Vanessa," he said. "Would it be convenient for you and me to discuss the matter tomorrow? It's of the utmost importance."

"Factory?" Vanessa said, forcing her eyes from Malcolm's. "Oh, yes, you did mention something about a factory being built here. I have no time to discuss it now, Simon. I have other things on my mind. I want to repair Bloodstone and will need your help and advice. But that too can wait." She glanced at the tall clock that stood against the wall. "It's late, and as long as you can't enlighten me with regard to the whereabouts of the bloodstone, I should be getting home. It has been a rather exhausting day."

"Let me walk with you," Malcolm said.

"You should be in your bed, Captain Drew," Simon put in. "I'll escort Vanessa back to Bloodstone. I'll hitch the carriage." He went toward the bell pull.

"No, that won't be necessary," Vanessa said quickly. "Please don't disturb your servants at this hour. I can walk it easily enough."

"And I would like to walk with you, if I may," Malcolm said.

"Thank you. That would be most pleasant."

Simon frowned. "I must insist," he said firmly. "It isn't safe for a young woman to walk at night."

"Not safe, Simon? Since when have the streets of Skull Point become unsafe?"

Simon looked flustered for a moment. "There are all kinds of new elements here since you left us five years ago, Vanessa. Things have changed. For the worse, I'm afraid."

"Yes, I must agree with you," Vanessa said pointedly. "

"Then by the gods in heaven you will not walk home alone," Malcolm vowed. "I insist upon escorting you."

"It would be much safer by carriage," Simon insisted.

"There is no one in Skull Point with whom I feel safe. Captain Drew has not yet involved himself in whatever dire politics is taking place here. I trust him, Simon," Vanessa said bitterly.

"My dear Vanessa," Simon gasped. "You're very much mistaken if you think I could do you any harm."

"And no harm will come to you from any source so long as I am with you," Malcolm said. "I'm sure Mr. Caldwell will permit me to hitch a rig and drive you home." He turned to Simon, who hesitated and then nodded.

"Good. Come then, Miss Vanessa...if I may be so bold as to call you Vanessa."

"You may be so bold," Vanessa said with a brilliant smile and a flippant toss of her head. "If in return I may call you Malcolm."

"Nothing would give me greater pleasure."

Simon was seething inside as the young couple left his house. He stood in the window and watched as they drove away. All the while his thoughts were on one thing: a method of getting rid of Malcolm Drew as quickly and as expediently as possible.

* * * * * * *

As they drove, Vanessa talked of Bloodstone, and of her

encounter with the sea captain and the bloodstone ring. She told Malcolm of the fairy story Tutrice had related and of the poem in the Bible and of her conviction that Malcolm's bloodstone ring was, in some way, the answer to that riddle.

Malcolm told her that he too felt a strange kinship with Bloodstone Manor, even though he'd never heard of it before. But as they neared the gates he looked up at the sagging old house and pulled the horse to a halt.

"Yes," he said. "I've seen it all before somewhere, in a dream perhaps."

"I should go in," Vanessa said. "It is rather late."

Malcolm came out of his reverie and helped her down from the carriage. Without realizing what he was doing, he pulled her against him, bending her body to fit into his own. He forced her head back.

Vanessa's first reaction was to resist him. Her mouth was open in protest. When he kissed her, she struggled, but only weakly. Then her arms moved up around his neck. She felt lost. She knew there would never be another man but Malcolm Drew.

Bloodstone, bloodstone out of the sea....

CHAPTER SIXTEEN

Vanessa felt like a butterfly emerging from its chrysalis. She could still feel the power of Malcolm's arms, the sweetness of his kisses, the heat of his passion. She'd never felt like this before. His words lingered in her ear. "Tomorrow," he had said. "Tomorrow, my beloved."

She didn't want to go in...not yet. The night was too glorious. She would never be able to sleep. She was too alive to sleep. She leaned against one of the tall, paint-flaked pillars of the veranda and looked out to the sea, the sea that had sent her love.

But, long ago that same sea had sent her another love. Would it be as before? Was life nothing more than one incident repeating itself again and again?

She remembered standing like this once before, many years ago. She had looked out to the sea then, as she was looking now, and had felt him standing beside her, tall and strong and protective.

Again she heard him say, "Come away with me, Vanessa. I love you more than life itself. I can't live without you."

She turned and touched his hand, running her palm over the massive red-black ring he wore. She felt the warmth of the stone, saw the love in his eyes and melted into his embrace.

"Yes, my dearest," she said. "I'll go with you to the ends of the earth."

"Hurry. Throw some things together and we'll leave tonight."

"No," she said, but not very emphatically. "My parents would never forgive me."

"I do not mean to dishonor you, Vanessa," he said. "Wake your old guardian. Let her come with us. We can be married in Boston."

Something nagged at Vanessa, telling her not to go with him. In the end, he left. Tutrice had been furious when she learned Vanessa had refused to accompany him.

"We must find him," Tutrice had said. "You must not let the bloodstone escape us. Hurry, child. We will follow him tonight."

At the height of a terrible storm, at an hour before midnight, Tutrice and Vanessa drove out of Skull Point, The wind was at their backs, goading them on. The search started in Boston, From Boston they traveled to Fall River, New Bedford, New London, back to Boston, Portsmouth, Salem. They went north to Penobscot Fay, south to Nantucket Sound. In Casco Bay they arrived just as his ship set sail for the Orient. He sailed out of her life, and her terrible dreams began.

Vanessa was too wrapped up in her memories and did not hear the door open behind her. "Are you never coming inside?" Tutrice asked. "Morning will be here before long."

Vanessa turned slowly. "What? Oh, yes. I'll be in shortly."

Tutrice came and stood next to her. "I see all has gone well. Did you find the bloodstone?"

"The bloodstone? No, I didn't find it," Vanessa said with a sigh.

Tutrice's smile faded. "You must find it," she said harshly.

"Oh, Tutrice. Let me be. I don't care about the bloodstone any more." Vanessa turned again to gaze out at the sea.

Tutrice grabbed her by the arm and pulled her around, "Don't care?" She searched Vanessa's face. "What has happened to you, child? You haven't let him escape you again?"

"No. He won't leave me this time, I assure you. Oh, Tutrice, he is so wonderful. I have never felt this way about any man. I have never really known what love is until tonight."

"He has made love to you?"

"We kissed," Vanessa admitted. "Oh, I do love him, Tutrice. I truly love him,"

"You felt that once before, remember?"

"No, never like this. It was the bloodstone that seemed important then. It wasn't the man. Now, all that is changed."

"You mustn't say that. The bloodstone *is* all that is important. The man is incidental."

"No. Malcolm means more to me than any ring could ever mean. I don't care about the ring. I wish I had never heard of it."

"Never say that again," Tutrice hissed. "You are the only one who can put things right for me."

"For *you*? What do you mean?"

Tutrice lowered her eyes. "I meant, for *us,* of course," she stammered, looking guilty.

"You said, for *you*," Vanessa said.

"It was merely a slip of my tongue."

"No." Vanessa tilted up the old woman's head and forced her to look into her eyes. "Everything I have done was at your insistence. Why is the bloodstone so important to you? It isn't for me at all, is it, Tutrice?"

"The bloodstone will benefit you, child," Tutrice managed to say. "Yes, I admit that my reasons for seeking it are selfish reasons. I cannot explain until the bloodstone is here."

"Well I'm not interested in your bloodstone any longer. Malcolm will be returning to the sea and I intend to go with him. I'll not stay here." She flung herself away from Tutrice and ran into the house and up to her room.

She cried because she felt she'd been betrayed all these years. She couldn't help it. All her life she had been pushed and prodded by the old woman. But never again, she vowed, as she sobbed into her pillow. Let the prophecy in the Bible go unfulfilled. She didn't care about it anymore. She didn't care about anything except Malcolm. One kiss, one simple embrace, and everything had changed.

And yet...she stemmed her tears and sat staring at the lamp that glowed dimly on the console. "Bloodstone, bloodstone out of the sea," she said. If it had not been for the bloodstone there would be no Malcolm, she thought. The bloodstone that brought him to her.

Never mind. She would go with Malcolm wherever he wished to take her. She would marry him and bear his children and live happily forever after. What did she care about a crumbling old house inhabited by a selfish crone and parents who wanted to be thought dead? This was no life for her. Her life lay with Malcolm Drew.

A tap at the door disturbed her troubled thoughts. The door swung easily on the well-oiled hinges. Jeremiah stood there in the threshold looking somber. "May I come in, daughter?"

Vanessa swung herself off the bed and swished her skirts around her. "Yes, please do. There are certain things I want to speak to you about, Father. Now is as good a time as any."

Her mood disturbed him. "It is late. Perhaps what we have to say to each other can wait until morning. I shouldn't have disturbed you." He turned to leave.

"No. There is no reason to wait. You most likely have come to tell me of more riddles. Or have you spoken to Tutrice?"

He nodded. "I spoke with her a few moments ago."

"What kind of fool have you all made of me?" Vanessa fumed. "I was shot at this evening. Someone tried to kill me on my way to Simon Caldwell's house. Was it your Doctor Smithers, Father? Was it the man who tried to kill you so that he would not have to repay an enormous debt he owed? Oh, I heard all the town gossip. I know why you're holed up here in this infernal house, afraid of your own shadows. But you sent me out without a word of warning. You set me up for someone else's vengeance."

"There is not much I can explain. You seem to know everything," her father said. He fanned out his hands. "But you were never in any real danger here at Skull Point. If you wish to think someone is trying to kill you, well, be that as it may. You are wrong, however. No one can harm you, Vanessa. Don't you see that?"

"What do you mean? Pushing me from cliffs and shooting at me are not exactly what I would look upon as acts of friendship."

Jeremiah made an unconcerned gesture. "I will admit that Doctor Smithers is indeed upset with me. But your mother and I are not hiding from him. We are here because we want no further dealings with the town. We prefer to be left to ourselves. There is a munitions factory to be built near this house—a factory some of the townspeople object to while others welcome it. I know that one word from me to the governor would stop that factory's construction, yet I refuse to give it. I am tired of the squabbles and wrangling amongst the people. I'm an old man, Vanessa—an old man who has been mixed up in the towns affairs for too many years. There comes a time when a man can stand just so much, then no more. But you, you need not fear any man. You need not be afraid of anything. I prefer to remain here and you should also. No one can harm you here."

"I don't agree," Vanessa said.

Jeremiah shook his head. "Well, no matter. You have always been a very obstinate girl. You have never been able to listen to reason. Think what you wish, child, I have no intention of swaying you one way or the other. You'll learn soon enough. But in the meantime, I must speak with you about this man."

"What of him?"

"Tutrice says you are in love with this Malcolm Drew?"

"Yes, I am," she admitted defiantly.

Jeremiah smiled faintly. "We have no serious objections to that, child. What we do have objection to is your disclaimer that you have no further interest in the whereabouts of the man's bloodstone ring."

Vanessa put her hands over her ears. "If I hear one more word about that accursed ring I shall lose my mind."

"Listen to me, Vanessa. You must find the ring. It is important to all of us."

"It is important to Tutrice. She as much as admitted that to me. All these years I have been used as a tool by that old woman. She dangled me as a lure on a line hoping to attract a man who wore a bloodstone ring on his hand. I don't even know why I permitted it. What significance that ring holds I don't know, nor do I care to know any more. I'm sick to death of it. I have found a man I truly love and I will go away with him, if he asks me... which I believe he will. I don't care about the bloodstone ring. I have myself to think about. I'll not be used any longer for your purposes or for the purposes of old Tutrice. I have a future and I intend to live it."

"You have an obligation. You are a Mallory. You must not forget that."

"And to what obligation do you refer?"

"The Justice Bible."

"I don't know what you are talking about."

"You know perfectly well. That prophecy must be fulfilled. You are the only person who can bring that bloodstone into this house." He had straightened himself to his full height and was glowering down at her. "After you have achieved that, then you will see where your future lies."

"My future lies with Malcolm Drew."

"Perhaps. But it is the ring that concerns us most. Your young man can only come second in your thoughts. You must get that ring."

"Malcolm will never come second to anything or anyone. He doesn't care about the ring and neither do I."

Jeremiah came to her and put his arm around her shoulder. "Then find the ring, child and bring it here. Restore it to its rightful place and then go to your young man, if you find you must. But first the ring, Vanessa. The bloodstone ring. It must be returned here or we will never be able to find peace of mind. We've given our promise." He looked imploringly into her eyes. "Please, my daughter. Do it for our sakes. Do it for your own sake. Find the bloodstone ring."

CHAPTER SEVENTEEN

Despite the few hours of sleep she'd gotten, Vanessa felt rested and eager to be away from Bloodstone.

The morning was as glorious as her mood. She would see Malcolm and they could make plans for their future together. She was certain he felt the same about her as she did about him. There had been something in the kiss that told her he loved her. No man had ever kissed her that way.

Again there was no one about when she left the house. She was glad of that. She did not want to face Tutrice or her parents. She had decided that she would do what she could about finding the bloodstone ring, but it would not be with the same determination she'd had earlier. If she found the ring, all well and good; but if not, well, Malcolm was all that mattered. She would do what she could for her family, for Tutrice, and then she was done with it.

Carl was in the driveway. She ordered him to saddle a horse for her. It would be a fine day for a ride.

* * * * * * *

The morning was calm and shiny as she galloped away from Bloodstone. It was early and the dew was thick on the grass and leaves. A cool but comfortable breeze blew in from the sea. Vanessa turned the horse toward town and galloped along the road.

It felt wonderful to be alive, letting the wind blow her hair, feeling the strength of the animal beneath her as it ate up the distance. She cut off the road and nosed the horse onto the path that led down to the beach. The salt water would be good for the hoofs.

At the water's edge she turned him sharply toward the left, spurring him faster and faster along the surf. She gave him free rein as they raced along, letting the sea air caress them, shortening the distance with each passing sound.

Malcolm was sitting on the steps at Simon's house, whittling a piece of wood. He jumped to his feet and came quickly to meet her. She had barely unsaddled herself before she found herself in his arms. His lips crushed over her mouth and his arms went around her. She kissed him hungrily, clinging to his strength, letting his passion melt into her own.

When their lips parted, he looked deep into her eyes. "Good morning, darling Vanessa," he said.

She smiled. "The townspeople will be scandalized," she said.

"Let them," he said. "Oh, Vanessa, Vanessa. I know it sounds insane—we only met yesterday—but I love you so very much. I never thought I would say that to a woman. I love you, Vanessa. I love you."

Simon Caldwell came out of the house in a rush. "Really, Vanessa. You are both behaving most improperly," he said indignantly. "Come inside at once."

Vanessa giggled, slipping her hand into Malcolm's. He laughed with her as they went past Simon and on into the house.

Once inside, they ignored Simon completely.

"Oh, Vanessa," Malcolm breathed, "I could not sleep for thinking of you. I was tempted to come to Bloodstone and carry you away." He pulled her into his arms again.

"I too couldn't sleep, Malcolm. I could hardly wait until morning to see you."

"I wanted to come to Bloodstone but Simon told me your father forbids anyone to set foot on his grounds. I had every intention of defying that order, however, if you did not come here."

Simon cleared his throat. "Vanessa, I must insist that you behave with a little more decorum. This man is a stranger to all of us."

"He is no stranger to me, Simon. I feel I've known him all my life."

"And I you," Malcolm sighed, pressing her fingertips against his lips.

Simon stood there scowling at them. "Brian will not approve of this, Vanessa," he said.

"Brian? What do I care what he approves of and what he does not? He has no claim on me."

"But you're practically engaged," Simon argued.

"I have never consented to marry Brian McGrath. It was he who assumed I would. I'll never marry Brian. I'll never marry anyone"—she turned to Malcolm—"but Malcolm Drew," she added.

"You are behaving most unwisely, both of you," Simon said. "You are rushing blindly into something you are too young to understand."

Malcolm smiled down at Vanessa. "We understand, Simon. We know that we are in love and that is all that is important."

"Fools. What is important is Skull Point...this town...the people...the belching factory that is planned on being built here." Simon's frustration was throwing him into a temper. "You don't think Skull Point is important, but where did you run to when things did not work out for you that last time, Vanessa?"

"How dare you?" she said.

"You went away before, Vanessa, and you came back. Well, if Skull Point becomes nothing more than a factory town, it will hardly be worth coming back to." He looked at Malcolm, who was staring at him, trying to understand what he was talking about. "Vanessa left us five years ago. She ran away with a man."

"That is not true. I did not run away with him. And you had best watch your tongue, Simon." She looked at Malcolm. "I told you about that last night. Tutrice and I went to search for the man who wore your bloodstone ring. He had asked me to elope with him, but I refused. Tutrice insisted that the ring he wore belonged at Bloodstone and we went to search for him in order to try to acquire the ring. Don't believe what this old fool says. He does not know what he is talking about."

"Sir," Malcolm said, his eyes cold. "I suggest you not try to slander Vanessa again. If you do, you will have me to deal with."

"Young fools. Selfish young fools." Simon went quickly toward the cabinet that stood against the wall. He took a key from his pocket and unlocked the top drawer and picked up the bloodstone ring. Turning round, he held the ring out to Vanessa.

She stared at it. "You had it all the time."

"I got it from Doctor Smithers. It was he who removed it from Malcolm's neck. It wasn't difficult to get him to give it to me. I offer it to you if you will stay here and help me with this factory problem."

"It is not yours to give, Simon. The ring belongs to Malcolm."

"Take it, my darling," Malcolm said. "I want nothing more to do with that ring."

Vanessa reached out and took the ring from Simon's hand. It felt heavy and hot in her hand. She suddenly hated the thing. She wanted nothing to do with the bloodstone ring. Yet she kept it and said, "Father will be pleased."

"And you will help me stop the building of the factory?" Simon said.

"I had intended to help in that regard from the very beginning," she told him. "Skull Point is no place for a munitions factory."

Simon gave a sigh of relief.

Vanessa's hand began to burn. She opened her fist and looked at the stone. It glowed up at her, as though it had a life of its own. The dazzling brilliance of its surface blinded her. The heat from the stone was so intense she found she could not hold onto it. With a sharp gasp of pain, she dropped the stone onto the carpet.

Simon thought of the Mallory lands, which she might try to take away from him. He picked up the bloodstone, turned, and redeposited it in the top drawer of the cabinet. "You may have the stone whenever you wish, Vanessa," he said. Of course he did not mean what he said. In exchange for the stone he would ask her to relinquish any claim she thought she had to the Mallory properties.

"I don't want it," Vanessa said, staring down at where the bloodstone had lain. "I never want to touch it again," she added, rubbing away the hurt in her hand. Malcolm took her hand and pressed his lips to the palm.

"Now you can understand my lack of interest in the ring. There is something evil about it," he said. "I'm glad you don't want it. When we met yesterday and you showed such a pronounced interest in the ring, I had intended to give it to you in repayment for saving my life. But now I'm glad you no longer want it, as I no longer want it. It has led me here to you. It has served its purpose. We don't need the ring any more, Vanessa. We have each other."

Simon made an uncomfortable sound in his throat again. "You will help me fight against this factory?" he said.

"Yes, Simon. I'll help you," she said impatiently. "What is it you want me to do?" She turned and faced him.

"I've called a meeting of the townspeople. I want you to speak to them. They believe I am fighting the factory for selfish reasons. There are a lot of them who want this factory. You will have to stand up to them alongside me. We might not be able to convince everyone that Skull Point is not the place for this factory, but we must get all the support we can. We must fight this thing, Vanessa. You can intercede with the governor. He knew your father. He'll listen to you."

"Perhaps, Simon. But how do we convince the townspeople that the factory should not be built here. I must agree that it will probably bring revenue into Skull Point."

"Together with a lot of unwelcome things. It will ruin our little town. Let them build their factory somewhere else. We must get the townspeople to see it our way."

Vanessa thought suddenly of what her father had said about

not wanting to bother with the town politics. She also thought of his lack of regard for her safety. She wanted to defy him. She wanted to get involved in the cause just to prove that she was a Mallory in the old sense of the name. She wasn't weak, like her father. "I'll do what I can, Simon," she said.

"I knew I could depend on you." He clapped his hands and rubbed them together enthusiastically. "Now. The first thing to be done is to meet with the people and try to rally them to see things our way. There will be many arguments. Everyone thinks I am opposed to the factory because it will mean having to give up lands that I—I mean, Skull Point—can put to better use. Come. Let us go down to the meeting. The people should be gathering just about this time."

Malcolm and Vanessa went hand in hand, not caring about the whispers all around them as they went through the crowd that had gathered in front of the general store. Brian McGrath's eyes were like twin daggers as he looked from Vanessa to Malcolm. He touched Vanessa's arm when she passed him, but she brushed past and went to stand next to Simon on the steps.

Simon raised his hands and yelled for the crowd to be quiet. "We all know why we are here," he said. "Miss Mallory has been intelligent enough to see things my way. She too is against building this munitions factory."

"How much did it cost you to get Mallory help?" someone yelled out.

Vanessa glowered and began scanning the sea of faces to determine who had spoken, but the man—whoever he was— melted into the crowd.

Vanessa stepped in front of Simon. "You people are foolish if you think the factory that is to be built here will help you or the town in any way. I have traveled. I have seen what factory towns turn into after a few years. The smoke and soot and dirt will kill your crops and taint your lungs. You women won't be able to hang your wash on the lines because of the grime and filth that the factory's chimneys will belch out. The air will become contaminated. The water will become contaminated by the silt and refuse they'll pour into our waters. This factory is for the manufacture of munitions, I understand. There will be the constant danger of explosion. The plant must not be built here. Are you all blind? Can't you see that?"

"All we see, Miss Vanessa," Josh Lancey said, stepping forward, "is that there are too many idle men in Skull Point. There's no work, no money. The factory will create jobs. We will be able to feed and clothe our families and ourselves. You don't know how bad things are around here since you went away, Miss Mallory. It's all well and good for Simon and the other people who have businesses to provide for them; but what about us common folk who have nothing? Noah Bingham don't make enough to provide all of us with work. He can hardly provide for Ruth and himself. The farms are not yielding anything. This has been a terrible last couple of years, Miss Mallory. Ever since your father...." He cut himself off. Instead he said, "We need work. We need that factory."

Vanessa raised her arms when everyone began clamoring and agreeing with Josh. "Listen to me," she called. When they became quiet again she said, "I realize that I have been away and may not be aware of the changes that have taken place in Skull Point. But I am back now and I will do everything I can to make Skull Point as prosperous as it once was."

"To do that you will have to take back the land from Simon Caldwell's control," someone yelled. It sounded like Ruth Bingham, Vanessa thought, but she didn't see the woman.

Again everyone agreed. Some shook their fists in Simon's direction.

"Well if that is what it takes, then I will do it," Vanessa said defiantly. "The businesses all flourished when my father was in control. If they have failed under Simon's control, then I will see to it that the Mallorys will again provide. The lands flourished under our hands. They will again. I promise you."

There was muttering in the crowd. Simon grabbed Vanessa's arm and turned her around. "You don't know what you're saying," he hissed.

She yanked her arm free. "There is no reason for these people to be in need," she said. "It was never that way before. If it is that way now, then you are to blame. My father did wrong to deed the properties to your control. I have every right to nullify that grant deed. It was made when they thought me dead. I believe any court of law would restore the properties to my name when they know the facts. You have always been a miserly man, Simon. I will help you stop the factory's construction; I will also take back what is mine."

In desperation Simon turned to the crowd. He made a motion to Will Wilkins and jerked his head toward Vanessa. Will Wilkins came forward. "You all know the girl is mad," he yelled. "Don't trust her."

"Mad, you say," Vanessa cried. She turned to the towns-people. "Think what you want about me, but think also of your empty stomachs and your unemployed men. Think of how diffi-cult things have been since Simon Caldwell decided to look out for your well-being. I may be mad, but I am not blind and I am a Mallory. We have looked out for Skull Point in the past. I can do it again."

And again the people muttered amongst themselves. Noah Bingham pushed himself to the front. "If you mean what you say, Miss Vanessa, I doubt if there would be a man, woman, or child who'd want to oppose you. Simon has not done well with the properties. Some of the farmers would like to have their farms, but they'll never have them so long as Simon holds the strings."

"I'll make a proposition to you all," Vanessa said. "Those who want title to their farms and businesses will have them if you will stand up with me and oppose this factory. After that, I will arrange to have the properties revert to Mallory control. With your help and the Mallory money we can restore Skull Point to the way it once was—prosperous and quiet and safe. Then I will let you buy your properties, those who wish to. I assure you I will make the prices well within your reach." She took Malcolm's hand. "I will not stay in Skull Point very long, and when I leave I would like to know that all my friends are happy and content and independent."

The people suddenly started to cheer her. Simon looked flushed with rage. He stepped down from the front of the general store and pushed his way through the crowd. When he passed Brian McGrath he motioned to him.

Brian hesitated. He glared at Malcolm Drew and tried to catch Vanessa's eye, but she had eyes only for Malcolm.

Brian turned angrily and followed Simon.

CHAPTER EIGHTEEN

"The people love you," Malcolm said as they walked along the lane leading Vanessa's horse. "And I love you. I didn't think I would ever say that to anyone. But I do love you, Vanessa... more than my life."

"And I love you, Malcolm...more than I can say."

He grinned. "It just isn't possible that all this has happened to me in so short a space of time. We have only met and here I find myself wanting desperately to marry you and take you away with me."

"And I will marry you, Malcolm...whenever you say."

"Tomorrow," he breathed. "Right now. Immediately."

Vanessa laughed. "That isn't possible, my darling. There is so much that must be done first. Preparations must be made. Announcements must be published. Invitations. Arrangements."

"Then we'll elope," he said, squeezing her hand.

"But I must keep my promise to the people of Skull Point. It shouldn't take long. After that we will go anywhere you wish just so long as we are together."

His expression went serious. "But I will be leaving in a few days," he said.

"Leaving?" She stopped and stared into his face. "When? For where?"

"My ship will be returning for me. When it does I must board it and be away."

"How long will it be before the ship arrives? How will they know where to find you? They more than likely think you are dead."

He shook his head. "They'll know I'm not dead. They'll find me, you can be assured."

"But you can't leave immediately. You mustn't. What about us?"

"I'll marry you. You can wait for me here. This will be our home on land."

"No, my darling. I want to go with you. I don't want to stay here alone. I couldn't bear to lose you now that I've found you."

"Then you will come with me. We will leave when the ship arrives at the harbor."

"But what if it comes too soon? I can't leave until I have fulfilled my promises to the people of Skull Point."

"Well, let's not worry about that now. Perhaps the *Sea Serpent* won't appear until after everything has been accomplished. Then we will board her together and go to our future."

Vanessa felt happy again. Things would work out this time. The old dreams would not come back. She would do what needed to be done at Skull Point. She would marry Malcolm and sail off with him when his ship arrived. And that would be a long time off, she hoped.

In the meantime there was the bloodstone ring to be considered. She did not know why the stone had repulsed her. She had spent the better part of her life searching for that ring and when it was handed to her she could not touch it.

She had to have it for her father's sake. She would have to touch it. She would have to get it from Simon and return it to Bloodstone. She would unravel the riddles, marry the man she loved and leave Skull Point forever. Her life seemed suddenly very orderly and she was happy, happy to the point of tears.

"You're crying," Malcolm said lovingly.

"I'm happy, Malcolm. Happier than I had ever thought possible."

He gathered her into his arms and kissed her passionately. "I will never let you be unhappy," he whispered. "I love you so."

Her resolve was shattered the moment she set foot inside

Bloodstone. There was something about her father's sober face, her mother's forlorn expression, Tutrice's anxiety, that made her heart sink. She felt as though the doors of a cage were swinging shut, separating her from the man she loved.

"You have the stone?" Tutrice asked, rushing up to her.

"No," Vanessa said.

"What do you mean? Is it still lost?"

"I know where it is," Vanessa said, resignedly. "Simon Caldwell has it. He took it from Doctor Smithers."

"Simon has the bloodstone?" her father asked.

"Yes. He offered it to me. I had it in my hand, in fact. But I could not hold onto it. It began to burn my skin. I dropped it. It is still in Simon's house."

"You dropped it?" Tutrice said, not believing her ears. "You dropped the bloodstone?"

"Yes, I dropped it." She shot Tutrice a look of defiance. "I couldn't touch the thing. Something inside me rebelled when I laid my hand to it."

"But that is not possible," Tutrice said. "You were fated to bring that stone back to this house. You *must* bring it back." Vanessa could see the alarm in her eyes. She looked very frightened.

Hester turned her eyes onto the old woman. "Perhaps you were wrong, Tutrice. Perhaps it is not Vanessa who was meant to return the bloodstone here."

"No, the signs were right. It was to be the last of the Mallorys."

Hester interrupted with, "But it may be that Vanessa will not be the last of the Mallorys. There is this man to be considered. What of her children?"

Tutrice thought for a moment. "No," she said after thinking. "The name is what is significant."

Vanessa stood looking from one to the other. She did not understand any of what they were saying, yet she kept still. She had lost interest in their squabble.

Hester said, "There is the possibility, however, that you were misled. You must try again, Tutrice. You must clarify the signs."

Tutrice frowned, then nodded. "Very well. Tonight."

Vanessa was barely listening to their exchange. She was standing there in body only. Her mind was with Malcolm. She wished he were here with her. No, not here...not in this house, she decided, and could not understand why she felt that way. She wanted him to be far, far away from Bloodstone, away from Skull Point. She would honor her promise to the local people, and then they would be gone, she and Malcolm together.

She left her parents and Tutrice muttering among themselves and went to the music room, closing the door after her. She wanted to be alone with her troubled thoughts.

She began thinking again of the first man who had worn the bloodstone ring, and of her old dreams...those nightmares that had plagued her for so long. Would Malcolm lead her to that same fate? Would he abandon her as the other man had abandoned her?

She found herself before the pianoforte. The lid was raised— as it always was—and on the music rack was a charming Mozart aria. She seated herself and ran her fingers over the polished keys.

"Dove sono i bei momenti," she sang in her soft lyric voice. "Where have they flown, those precious moments?" Were the precious moments with Malcolm ended?

Suddenly she banged her hands down on the keys and slammed the lid shut. She would not permit this strange gloom to torment her. She got up from the pianoforte and went quickly out of the music room. The foyer was empty now; there was no sign of Tutrice or her parents. She was glad of it. She wanted to be out of this house.

She flung the front door open and went out into the dwindling light of the late afternoon. Her horse was still hitched to the post where she had left him. Without forethought she leaped into the saddle and galloped down the drive.

Rather than turning toward Skull Point and Malcolm, she— or something else—tugged the reins to the left and she galloped off in the opposite direction.

The sun was beginning to rest on the horizon when Vanessa reined up at the edge of the bluff. She looked down at the crashing surf and thoughts of the danger she'd encountered at the edge of the cliff washed over her.

She tugged the reins and pulled the horse back and around and started off in still another direction. She was not conscious of how far she had ridden or to where. Her thoughts were on Bloodstone and her family...on Malcolm and the people of Skull Point. She thought of Simon and Brian, admonishing herself for having led him to believe she was mad. If she had not played that childish game with Brian, the townspeople would have been easily rallied to her side.

She stopped the horse with an incautious tug of the reins and realized that she'd been daydreaming and had come quite a long, long way from Bloodstone and the town. There were no houses in sight, no familiar landmarks. Yet she did not feel afraid. The path was wide and smooth and well-trodden so she was not exactly lost. She would ride on and eventually come to some cottage where they would direct her. She would find herself home in time to meet Malcolm.

She brought the horse to a trot, letting him have more or less his own head. The sun was sinking out of sight and heralding its departure was a fine, cold mist that drifted in from the sea. Straight ahead Vanessa saw the tall lofty shape of a bluff. She thought she recognized it; and as she watched, the rolling blanket of fog crept up over it and swallowed it completely.

The horse began to stir uneasily as the fog grew thicker. For the first time, Vanessa felt genuine concern. The fog was creeping around her all too quickly, blotting out all traces of trees and rocks and landscape.

She tried to remain calm and reminded herself that there was nothing to fear. She went slowly, being careful not to let the horse set its own pace now. The fog was too thick and they could easily come across another bluff and fall over its edge.

Why had she come so far? Why hadn't she taken a cloak and a hood? Her riding habit suddenly felt very thin and scanty.

The cold was chilling her bones. Her arms began to ache from holding so tight a rein on the horse. Dampness settled on her brow; her eyes hurt as she strained to see through the gathering cloud of grey.

They went on for what seemed hours. She heard nothing except the pounding of her heart in her breast and the soft clip-clop of the horse's hoofs on the damp ground. A sudden chill of fright went through her as she listened to the horse's hoof beats. The sounds of the hoofs was suddenly more muffled than before and Vanessa realized with a sinking heart that somehow they had managed to leave the path and were traveling over sodden earth. She looked down and confirmed that the path had vanished. She knew she was lost but did not want to admit it to herself.

The horse felt skittish beneath her. She almost collided with a thick oak tree. She reined again uncautiously and the horse reared. She slapped him smartly with her hand and told him to be quiet. The sound of her own voice amid the thick mist sounded eerie and unearthly. The words drifted into a muffled blur.

She had to stay rational. It might be worthwhile to dismount and travel on foot. She would feel safer trusting her own steps rather than the horse's. And, if she did step into a bog or slip over a steep bluff she would have the horse's reins tightly in hand to save herself.

But on foot she would be at the mercy of rocks and land-holes, snakes and other dangers. The horse was solid beneath her; the ground might not be so solid. Besides, walking would be tiring, although she had to admit that it would help warm her if she were moving under her own power. The mist was thicker and colder and her skin was chilled clear through.

It happened all too quickly. An owl screeched...or was it a human voice that frightened the horse? The thick fog distorted the sound and made it impossible to locate. Vanessa started and the horse bolted. It kicked its forelegs up into the air. Vanessa fell backward. She banged her head on something solid and everything went black for a moment.

How long she lay in a daze she did not know, but when she came to her senses she found herself quite alone. The horse had run off into the fog and Vanessa was at the mercy of the elements. Luckily the ground on which she fell was soft enough not to injure her.

She felt around. She had hit her head on a fallen branch, but other than a dull headache, she seemed to be unharmed. She brushed herself off and got to her feet. She knew that they could not have traveled too far off the path. It had to be somewhere near.

She stood and tried to remember in which direction they'd been facing when the alarming sound caused the horse to bolt. She had lost her bearings. She took a step and her foot came down on the fallen branch.

If she had fallen backward—as she had—and her head had collided with the branch, then they had obviously been headed in that direction, she told herself, pointing. They more than likely had merely angled off the path. She started back, feeling sure that her reasoning was correct.

She went far, however, without finding the path. She walked until her legs ached and her feet felt like blocks of ice. The cold was becoming more and more severe. She would have to find shelter soon.

She stumbled and rolled down a slight slope, coming to rest after a few yards. The ground was sandy and in the distance she could hear the muffled roar of the surf. She was on the beach, then, but what beach?

Again she got to her feet, this time a little less steadily. She walked forward until her shoes sank into the wet, soggy sand. She was at the water's edge, but she could not see the wide expanse of water. She saw nothing but a heavy gray blanket that hung all around her.

She started back in the direction from which she'd come. She stumbled over rocks and tangles of seaweed. Her riding habit was wet, now, and heavy. Through a fleeting break in the fog she saw the mouth of a cave. It was high up in the bluff but there seemed to be a man-made path leading to it.

The rough, wide-mouthed cave would offer a kind of shelter. She could wait there until the fog lifted. She'd be safe, at least for the moment. And Malcolm would come searching for her when she did not keep their appointed rendezvous. He would find the horse and it would lead him to her.

Feeling less afraid, she started to climb.

CHAPTER NINETEEN

The cave's safety proved illusory.

Just inside its mouth, clinging to the slime-coated roof, were hordes of bats. Vanessa was well inside the cave when she saw them, and when she did, she screamed, and the startled bats came away from the roof of the cave in great swarms.

Covering her head with her hands, she ran deeper into the cave, but when she looked back she saw that the bats had swooped out through the mouth of the cave, and vanished into the fog. She leaned her head against the cave's rough wall and tried to bring her breathing back to normal.

She heard voices, far away and indistinct. They were coming from the very bowels of the tunnel. She cocked her ear and tried to listen. It was as though someone or something was moaning, yet the moans had a rhythm, a pattern to them.

Not moans, she decided—chants. She inched herself forward in the direction of the sounds.

The tunnel angled right and up ahead she saw a glimmer of light. The chanting was louder here. The floor of the cave began to slope upward, gradually at first, then more steeply before it leveled off. Huge boulders stood on either side of her and when she eased herself around one of them she found herself on a ledge in the mouth of a tiny opening that looked down upon a vast cavern.

At first the figures that moved and the fire that burned held her spellbound. Then after her initial surprise, she studied the figures and the voices and a gasp caught in her throat.

A huge fire was blazing before an altar of skulls. A wave of nausea ripped through Vanessa, but it was not only the pile of skulls that repulsed her, it was the figures. They were stark naked, with the exception of three. Those three she knew very well.

Tutrice, Hester, and Carl stood before the skulls, which were piled high to form a kind of altar. They looked grotesque and indescribably sinister. All three stood tall above the others, who were huddled naked on the floor, body to body, some crouching, others prostrate. She saw her father among them...and Clarissa.

The central figure was Carl, dressed in a flowing white muslin vestment, with a high crown on his head and a black cape thrown across his shoulders. His eyes were covered by a mask of the most bizarre design. His face was all painted with horrible lines and colors. His mouth was made wider at the corners by bright red marks that curved down the edges of his lips. Between his teeth was held a long, golden rod.

Tutrice was not garishly dressed; she wore her usual bombazine dress, but in her hands was a heavy black sack. From time to time she would dip her hands into the sack and bring forth some thick, running matter which she threw upon the heap of skulls.

Vanessa's mother, Hester, stood to the other side of Carl. She was dressed—if one could call it dressed—in a thin, filmy gown so transparent Vanessa blushed with shame. She was poised, motionless as a statue with her arms thrust forward. In her hands she clutched what to Vanessa looked like a flask of some kind and a bludgeon. She kept her feet planted well apart, her head thrown back. There was a sort of shameless abandon in the whole posture of her body.

The three stood before the altar of human bones in the dull smoky light, while the huddled, groaning, groveling figures of the others lay prostrate before them on the dirt floor.

Vanessa cowered against the wall. She did not want to watch the hideous spectacle before her eyes, but felt transfixed, unable to tear her eyes away.

"I am here, O great and majestic father," she heard Carl call out. "My eyes are blanked with death. Oh, come to your son, father of darkness. We implore you to come amongst us."

A huge draft of smoke rose from the fire. Vanessa looked toward it, expecting a shape to appear in the fire. None appeared, yet she heard an unworldly sound that seemed to rattle the very core of the earth. The whole place shook. The ground trembled, the walls seemed to breathe in and out.

"One of your children needs your light," Carl chanted.

Tutrice stepped forward, turning her eyes into the flames. Across the distance separating them, Vanessa saw those eyes—wide and red and glowing with fire. "Vengeance has not fallen," she said. "She has refused the bloodstone."

A cold sweat broke out on Vanessa's skin. She could feel it beading on her forehead. She began to tremble, knowing to whom Tutrice referred.

Again there was a shaking of the earth, a rattling of the walls and floor and ceiling. Again the smoke puffed up and a low, grumbling noise was heard.

Tutrice bowed low and stepped back away from the fire.

The naked figures on the ground began to writhe and sway and moan.

Vanessa could not watch the hideous proceedings any longer. She put her hands over her eyes, but she could still hear the dreadful groans that seemed to answer Carl's plea, a series of deep, rasped gutturals, strung together on meaningless vowel monotones. To Vanessa it sounded like a prolonged death-rattle. She sank to her knees and fell forward in a dead faint.

* * * * * * *

At first, when she opened her eyes, she could not remember where she was. She was lying on her side and all she could see was the hard, rough ground and darkness everywhere. Gradually, she began to remember, but there were no sounds now, only an ominous silence. Below, the fire was still smoldering, but the cavernous room was empty.

She had to get out. The place was evil, a site for devil worship. But she could not go back the way she had come, to the unknown beach.

If Tutrice and the others had entered the cavern, there must be a tunnel other than the one Vanessa had entered through. She looked across the expanse and saw a passageway cut into the solid wall opposite her.

Beneath her, rocks jutted from the wall of the cave. She thought they would allow her access to the chamber below, and from it she could take the other tunnel.

She stiffened her courage and eased herself over the side of the ledge. Carefully she put one foot onto the first jutting stone nearest the ledge. She tested it for strength and finding it capable of holding her weight, she shifted her body from her perch.

She looked down and saw her next footing. Holding fast to the lip of the ledge she reached for it with her foot. The stone was as sturdy as the first. She lowered herself, then clung to the wall, accustoming herself to her precarious predicament.

Forcing her courage she stepped downward until her foot touched still another jutting rock. Again she tested it for its strength and again found it strong enough to support her. She lowered herself down, step by painstaking step, moving her body nearer and nearer the floor of the cavern. She worked closely, silently, nervously.

Suddenly the rocks ran out. She tried to cling to the wall where she was, but her strength gave out and she fell—but not so far as to harm herself. She felt herself to make sure she had no broken limbs. Her riding habit was torn, but that was not of any importance. She was safe...at least for the moment.

She picked herself up and skirted the fire, keeping her eyes averted from the pile of human skulls, which glowed as though covered with phosphorus. The eerie light they emitted sent chills up and down her spine. She refused to let herself think of how they got here. Were they pirate bones, or of a more recent vintage?

She made her way toward the opposite tunnel. When she reached it she found the air much fresher. The tunnel seemed wider and more traveled. The flooring was smoother and less cluttered with rocks and boulders. An uncomfortable, acrid smell permeated the passageway as she went along it. It was dark, but her eyes were growing accustomed to that, which made her going easier and faster.

The air became fresher and cooler. Before a half-hour had passed she found herself standing under a black night sky. Swirls of fog lingered here and there in patches. She could see the outline of trees, tall and black. She recognized a pile of rocks.

She was to the south of Bloodstone. The path directly to her left would take her home. Quickly she searched it out. She breathed a sigh of relief when she found it and turned herself in the direction of home.

As she went she thought it very strange that in all her years she had never once come across the entrance to that cavern. She had never known it existed. She had been an inquisitive child and was constantly falling into mischief because of her desire to explore. How odd that she had never found that cave!

Bloodstone loomed before her. It looked blacker and more ominous as she walked toward it. The strange mist that had swept in so quickly was beginning to evaporate up into the night. As she passed through patches of it, it swirled up around her, finally dissolving into nothing.

Vanessa was chilled through. Her muscles ached, her head throbbed painfully. Yet the sight of Bloodstone gave her the courage to go on. She felt that, once inside its portals, she would again be safe and secure and nothing would be able to harm her.

But she hesitated when she thought of having to confront Tutrice and her parents and Carl. What had they been about? She knew well enough that Tutrice enjoyed practicing the voodoo arts she'd learned as a child among the Cajuns. How could she face her mother or father? She had seen their shameful exhibition and remembering it made her wince with disgust.

It had been Carl who had called himself son of the father of darkness. She knew only too well who was known as the father of darkness. How could her parents permit themselves to become enmeshed in such voodoo nonsense?

Vanessa paused at the back door, hearing voices from inside the house. One of the voices was that of Carl; the other voice belonged to Tutrice. Carl's voice sounded as angry and upset as Vanessa felt.

"You have always tried to go against me," she heard Carl say. "I have told you time and time again that you can no longer protect that child. She is what she is and you must not put yourself in front of her again."

"She is entitled to a life of her own," Tutrice argued. "We cannot keep her a prisoner in this place. She is too young. She needs to find life and happiness...a life of her own, not ours."

"It is too late for that now," Carl said angrily. "You have defied us for the last time, Tutrice. You heard the father tonight. He is not pleased with your interference."

She heard Tutrice moan and begin to sob. "I meant no harm," the old woman said. "I only wanted her to be happy."

"You should not have done what you did. You have angered him and for that you will be punished."

"I don't care what you do to me," Tutrice said, continuing to sob. "Do what you wish, but do not force that young child into something she is not."

Vanessa stood silent and stiff. She leaned forward, intent upon entering the house, but something held her back.

"It was made clear," Carl said, "Vanessa is the one who must bring the bloodstone to this house. Why we are doing all this for you, I do not know. You hardly deserve it after what you have tried to do."

"I have been faithful. There have been many years of loyal service which I have gladly donated," Tutrice said.

"Perhaps it is because of your past loyalties that this is being done for you. But once this is accomplished, our debt to you is finished and your powers will cease to exist. You have done wrong, Tutrice, and you will pay for it."

"I did what I felt I had to do," Tutrice said. "I love the child more than life itself. She does not belong here. She should be given a life of her own," she repeated.

"You know that that is not possible. She herself brought about her situation. We had nothing to do with it."

"But it was only by accident."

"Accident? Impossible. There is no such thing as an accident insofar as we are concerned," Carl argued.

"But what of her parents?" Tutrice begged. "What is to become of them?"

"You ask that now?" Carl asked, sounding more annoyed and disgusted. "It was you who insisted justice must fall. That is what you asked and you are receiving it. What sort of forked-tongue creature are you?"

Again Tutrice moaned and sobbed. "I want no harm to come to any of them."

"It is too late for that now," Carl said. "But I can assure you all will be right. Light will be dark and days will be night... vengeance will rest with bloodstone and wife. That is what we promised and that is what will come about."

Then Vanessa heard her father's voice. "We have done what you've asked, Carl," he said. "What more do you want of us?"

"You will be told what you need to know in time," Carl said. "I do not think anything more will be required. You will be able to leave Bloodstone soon, if you wish. The people of the village will accept you without question, as they accepted me and Clarissa. But kindly remember that Vanessa must be responsible for bringing the bloodstone here. Once that is accomplished, everything will be put right and our obligation will be paid."

Hester spoke up, saying, "But vengeance cannot fall through Vanessa. You have all misunderstood what was said."

"Dear Hester," Carl said patiently. "Do you mean to tell me I did not understand the voice of my own father?"

Vanessa could not stand to listen to another word. She grabbed the knob and swung open the door, storming into the kitchen—and stopped dead in her tracks.

The kitchen was empty.

CHAPTER TWENTY

The entire house was empty.

She felt as though she were losing her mind. She'd heard them quite clearly. She hadn't dreamed it. True, she was exhausted from her ordeal in the fog and again in the cave, but she could not have been mistaken about the conversation she had over-heard. But how could she have heard them talking? There was no one in the house...no one.

She sat down on the lower step of the staircase and put her head in her hands. She longed to be with Malcolm. At least he would help her retain her sanity. It wasn't possible to hear voices that weren't there. Was it possible that the terrible ritual in the cave had been some kind of wild hallucination? Had her fall and the blow on her head caused her to imagine the whole awful episode? It was all too impossible. Carl had led those demonic rites in the cavern. There was some kind of ugly, unnatural bond between him and her family.

Memory made her gasp. Clarissa had been there. "But that was impossible. I couldn't have seen her," she told herself.

She had to get out of Bloodstone. Tired as she was, she had to leave this house and run to Malcolm. He would know what to do. He would be able to protect her from this evil she'd stumbled upon. She would change into dry, clean clothes and go to him.

She ran up the stairs and into her room, locking the door out of fear. As she stripped, the dampness seemed to lift itself from her skin and she seated herself on the side of the bed. Her head fell into her hands again and she started to weep. She was terrified by the unknown powers that were all around her. She threw herself across the bed, crying into her pillow—and fell asleep.

When she awoke the sun was streaming in through the broken shutter. Then she remembered, the whole horrible scene of the previous night.

She pulled on fresh clothes and tidied herself as quickly as she could. She had to get out of Bloodstone and never return to this terrible place.

The house was still empty when she went down the stairs and out the front door. She felt weak with hunger but she would take breakfast in Skull Point.

Outside, grazing on the overgrown front lawn, was the horse that had bolted and thrown her from the saddle. When he saw her he raised his head and whinnied. She hurried to him, not caring whether she wore habit or not, and mounted. She kicked the horse into motion and galloped as fast as she could down the drive and toward Skull Point.

The day felt fresh and clean in contrast to the dismal atmosphere of Bloodstone. As she went down from the bluff, galloping over the sweeping curve of the road, she suddenly pulled on the reins, bringing the horse to a halt. She saw the tiny harbor, but something was different. A ship was anchored in the bay. Its sails were secured as it sat at rest. She felt that she'd seen the ship before. It looked vaguely familiar. It was painted a dark red with black trimmings. She couldn't make out the name, but she knew it instinctively. It would be the *Sea Serpent*—Malcolm's ship. She was positive of it.

Again she spurred the horse on, giving him free rein. Her hair streamed out behind her as she went like the wind. Malcolm's ship was here to take him away. He must not go. He could not go...not yet...not now. There was so much to be settled before they left.

She didn't go to Simon's house as she had intended. If the ship were here, Malcolm would be at the wharf, or aboard it already. She steered the horse in that direction.

He was standing amid bales and crates and boxes piled near

the pier. He had a register in his hand and was giving quick, sharp orders to a group of sailors who scurried around him. When he saw her, he lowered the register and went smiling to meet her.

She jumped down from the horse and ran into his arms. She had not intended to, but she began to cry again.

"Vanessa, darling, what is it?" he asked, looking at her with concern. "You didn't keep our appointment last night," he said trying to calm her.

The sailors had stopped their work and were watching them.

"Come, darling," Malcolm said, leading her away from the inquisitive faces of the men. He took her around a pile of bales, seated her on one of them and offered her his handkerchief. "What is it, Vanessa? What's troubling you?"

"It was so horrible, Malcolm," she sobbed.

"What? What was horrible?"

In sobbing, choking breath she told him about becoming lost in the fog, finding the cave, seeing Carl and the altar of skulls. "And when I returned to Bloodstone," she continued, sobbing, "They were in the kitchen talking about me. They were arguing...my parents, Tutrice and that terrible Carl. They said I must be responsible for bringing the bloodstone back to Bloodstone Manor. Oh, Malcolm," she wailed, throwing herself again into his arms. "I want no part of it. I want to get away from that place."

He patted her lovingly. "Then that is what you will do," he said. "The *Sea Serpent* arrived early this morning. We have but to take on provisions and we will be ready to set sail with tomorrow morning's tide. I will take you away from all this. We will be married today. Simon is a judge, is he not? He will be able to perform the ceremony."

"Oh, yes, Malcolm. Take me away. Take me away."

"Come, my darling. Don't cry any more. I'll protect you from whatever wickedness you believe exists in Bloodstone."

She stiffened. Through her tears she looked into his face. "You don't believe me," she said. "You think I imagined what I said I saw?"

He smiled. "Of course I believe you. If you said you saw those devil worshipers, then I believe you saw them."

"You're humoring me," she said, studying his expression. "You don't believe me. You think I'm crazy too, don't you?"

"Of course I don't. I love you, Vanessa. That is all that matters."

"That is not all that matters. I am not crazy, Malcolm. I did not imagine everything I told you. I saw them. I saw them with my own eyes. It was horrible...."

"There, there, my love. Don't upset yourself. Come. We'll find Simon and ask him to perform the ceremony. Come along."

"No. I can tell by your eyes that you think me mad. I'm not mad. You've been listening to what the others are saying about me and you believe them."

"Vanessa, speak sensibly. Would I want to marry you if I thought you to be mad?"

"You might. I know nothing about you. Oh, I don't know what to think any more. I don't trust anyone."

"You trust me, don't you?"

"I don't know," she admitted after a moment's hesitation.

"I love you, Vanessa," Malcolm said, standing up. "If you don't choose to believe that, then I am very sorry. I want you to come away with me. I want to marry you. What more proof do you need of my love?"

"What of them?" she said aloud and Malcolm frowned at her. "My parents, Tutrice, the people of Skull Point?"

"Vanessa," He said, laying a hand on her shoulder and bringing her out of her reverie. "Please come away with me. Let's go to Simon and have him marry us. We can sail on the morning tide."

"Simon?" she said in a faint voice. "Yes. He has the bloodstone. We will go to Simon. I will return the bloodstone and all will be righted."

Malcolm frowned again as he heard her speak as if in a trance. "Forget the bloodstone," he said. "Let them have it. If it belongs to Bloodstone then let Simon take it there."

"No, I'm responsible. I must go to Simon," she said, as if speaking to herself.

"We'll go together," Malcolm said.

"I must go to Simon. The bloodstone. I must take the bloodstone home." She started away from him. Malcolm gripped the reins of her horse and followed behind, wondering suddenly if perhaps what they were saying about Vanessa were indeed true.

One of the sailors working with the crates called to Malcolm. "We must get this gear loaded, Captain," he said.

Malcolm hesitated. He looked at the register in his hand and the ship that sat at anchor in the bay. Vanessa was walking ahead. He caught up with her. "Darling," he said hurriedly. "You go ahead. I'll meet you at Simon's. Wait for me there. I will only be a few moments. These provisions must be checked carefully. We have a long voyage ahead of us. I'm the only one responsible."

"The only one responsible," Vanessa said. It was as if she had not heard him at all.

Malcolm put the reins of the horse into her hand, patted her affectionately on the cheek and turned back to his men who were working the bales and crates. "I'll only be a short while," he called as Vanessa turned and started toward Simon's house.

Brian was standing in the driveway when Vanessa appeared. She was staring straight ahead of her, looking neither right nor left. When she passed, not seeing him, Brian took her arm. "Vanessa, you are looking so strange. What's the matter?"

"Nothing," she said softly. "I must see Simon."

"He is not at home. I've just knocked. The maid said he has gone down to Devon to talk with the mayor. He is going to try talking them into allowing the munitions factory to be built there instead of here at Skull Point. Fat chance he has, though. Those Devon people are less industrial-minded than anyone. They'll never permit a factory to be built on their premises."

Vanessa walked away from him, going toward Simon's front door.

"Vanessa?" Brian said, taking her by the arm again. "I've just told you, Simon isn't at home." He looked at her and saw the strange light in her eyes. "What's wrong with you? You look very odd." When she did not answer he said, "Is it that man? Has he wronged you in any way?"

"Man?" she said, turning to him. She blinked. "Brian? What are you doing here?"

"Vanessa, something is wrong. Tell me what it is. Let me help you."

"Nothing is wrong, Brian. I've come to see Simon for the bloodstone ring. Malcolm is leaving on the morning tide. We're to be married."

"Married? No. I can't permit that," Brian said, aghast.

"We do not need your permission," Vanessa said haughtily. "We will ask Simon to marry us and I will go with Malcolm when his ship sails in the morning."

"But you can't. You can't leave Skull Point. Remember the promises you made to the people yesterday? You must stay. They are depending on you. You mustn't leave."

"But I must, Brian. I can't explain, but I must get away from Bloodstone or something terrible will happen to me."

"What could happen to you?"

"Something terrible, that's all I know. I can't say exactly what, but I know I must get away from here as quickly as I can. I must return the bloodstone ring to my parents and then I must leave."

"No, please, Vanessa. Think for a moment. You can't desert your family, your friends, your home...just for a man you barely know."

"Oh, Brian, you are a sweet and charming man, but don't you understand? I feel I've known Malcolm all my life, longer than you even. We were meant for each other. I knew that the moment I saw his face. I love him. I need him. I want to spend the rest of my life with him."

"How could you love him? You don't know him. For all you know he might be taking you to some god-forsaken land where civilization has never been heard of."

"I don't care where he takes me, just as long as he takes me. There can never be any other man for me, Brian. Never. I know that now."

"Then you've never loved me," he said sadly.

"I'm sorry, Brian. No, I've never really loved you. Oh, I'm fond of you, of course. I'll always have a special place in my heart for you, but I could never marry you."

"I've always tried to give you what you wanted," he said. "If this Malcolm Drew is what you want, then I guess I have no other alternative but to step aside. But first, Vanessa, think about Skull Point and your home. The factory people are due tomorrow afternoon. Can't you stay long enough to stand up with the people of the town? If you sail on the morning tide, they'll think you deserted them and they will welcome the factory. Stay until tomorrow night. Stay and help us fight off the construction of this factory. Please, Vanessa. Help us. Help the people who have always loved you. Don't run out on us when we need you most."

"Oh, Brian," Vanessa sobbed, "I must go with him. If I don't sail with him I'll lose him, can't you see that?"

"And if you go with him, you'll lose us—the people who love you most. The people who have always been loyal."

"Please don't try to shame me, Brian. I must do what I must do. I can't help the way I feel. Don't stand in the way of my happiness. Please let me sail on the morning tide."

Brian shook his head. "I could never refuse you anything. I did not mean to shame you, Vanessa. Of course you must go, if that is what will make you happy. I would not be truthful if I said I believe it will make you happy. You left us once before, remember? I know I am being a cad to bring it up, but I must try to make you see reason."

"My mind knows no reason. What is reason anyway? I'm ruled by my heart, Brian. I've always been ruled by it. It is the only thing I know. Say you will wish me luck and happiness. Tell me you are not angry with me."

He smiled down at her. "I could never be angry with you, Vanessa. I will always love you; you know that. Go, if that is what you feel you must do. Be happy."

"Oh, Brian, thank you," she gushed, throwing her arms around his neck. "I'll never forget you. Never."

"One thing before you go." Brian hesitated and felt the color redden his cheeks. "Kiss me one last good-bye, Vanessa. Please."

Her eyes were brimming with tears. "Oh, Brian. Dear, sweet, wonderful, Brian," she said and felt his arms go around her and his lips cover hers. In gratitude she tightened her embrace and kissed him long and lovingly.

They did not see Malcolm Drew standing watching them. There was fire in his eyes. He moved quickly. He grabbed Brian's shoulder and spun him around. His fist connected with Brian's jaw. Brian fell unconscious on the first punch. Vanessa screamed, wide-eyed with alarm. Malcolm's rage was uncontrollable. Before he knew what he was doing, his hand slashed out and he slapped her across the face.

"You two-faced vixen," he snarled.

He turned and strode away.

CHAPTER TWENTY-ONE

Alone in her bedroom at Bloodstone, she berated herself for not running after him—all for stupid pride.

He had seen things as they were on the surface and had accepted them on face value. She had to remind herself, though, that she was as much a stranger to him as he was to her. She should have run after him and explained the kiss. Brian meant nothing to her. Malcolm should have known that. But he didn't know her; nor did she know him.

She paced the room, not knowing what to do. There was no one to ask for advice. Her parents seemed to have vanished into thin air. Tutrice was not there. There was no one she could turn to. In the morning he would be gone. She would lose him.

He mustn't leave without her. She would go to him and explain. She would make him understand.

She donned a long cape with a hood and went out of the house. The night was cold and a strong wind was blowing in from the sea. The sky was black with clouds. There would be another storm.

Not a sound was heard except the howling of the wind that lashed at her as she made her way along the road. The way to Skull Point looked as though nobody had been that way for hundreds of years. Huge, towering trees hugged the road, blocking her view of the open sea. There were no shadows; there was no moon. Except for the moaning of the wind, an eerie quiet hung over everything.

She took a path that led through a tangle of overgrowth. She wanted to see the bay. She wanted to be sure the *Sea Serpent* was still lying at anchor. At first, when she reached the bluff, she saw nothing below but darkness. Then, faint and indistinct in the night, she saw the glimmer of light, a tiny speck, flashing and blinking in the bay. The ship was still there, readying itself for its morning voyage. She turned back into the tangle of over-growth and quickened her steps.

A twig snapped nearby. She drew herself up and looked behind her, but saw nothing. She began to walk faster. The path was softer underfoot. She was walking on moss, she thought. The path seemed to have disappeared. Another sound brought her up again. She strained to listen but heard only the sighing of the wind through the trees. Again she went on. If someone was here in the wood with her, she did not want to encounter him.

There was something sinister abroad this night. She wanted to get to Malcolm and convince him of her love for him. Nothing could deter her from her purpose. Her goal was the *Sea Serpent* and nothing, not even the devil himself, would keep her from reaching that ship.

Suddenly a shape took form directly in front of her. It was the silhouette of a man. Vanessa gasped and clutched her throat.

"Good evening, Miss Vanessa," a voice said. It was a voice she knew. She strained, but could only see the man's outline. His figure was as familiar as his voice.

"Who are you? Come closer," she said.

The man chuckled. She did not like the sound of it. "I have been wanting to talk with you again," the man said.

"Doctor Smithers? Is that you?"

"Yes, it is I," he said, stepping closer. In the darkness she saw his features, but faintly.

"You gave me a fright," she said, trying to keep herself calm. She knew that this was a man to fear, if everything she'd heard about him was true. "I was on my way to see Malcolm Drew. He is planning to sail on the morning tide."

"So I heard," Doctor Smithers said. He came closer and Vanessa saw his face. He was smiling a strange smile. His eyes looked glassy; they made her think of another pair of eyes. "Too bad you are not traveling with the young captain," the doctor said.

"But I am," Vanessa answered. "Malcolm has asked me to marry him. I will sail with him tomorrow."

"No, Vanessa. You cannot leave here. You will never leave Skull Point. Your place is here with your parents and that old guardian. You'll not leave. I can't permit that."

"You sound like Brian. He said something similar. I'll tell you, as I told him, that I do not need your permission. I will do what I please and no one, not you or anyone else, is going to stop me."

Suddenly he reached for her and grabbed her wrists. He moved so unexpectedly that she did not have time to back away. He held her tight and began pulling her along after him as he turned and walked away. Vanessa struggled, but his grip was stronger than she thought it could be.

"Let me go," she yelled, suddenly frightened more than she cared to admit. She scratched and clawed at his hand, but he held her fast and continued to drag her after him. "Let me go, I tell you."

Doctor Smithers dragged her into a clearing. He pulled Vanessa close and peered into her face. She detected the smell of alcohol on his breath. "You will never leave Skull Point," he said. He gave her a quick, hard shove forward.

Vanessa's feet sank into damp, thick moss. She tried to step back but something was holding her feet solidly implanted in the mossy ground. She tried to get out of it, but could not.

"I can't move.... My feet...."

"This bog will be your tomb, Vanessa. You'll be the last I have to contend with."

She saw the same evil gleam in his eyes that she had seen in Carl's. She could not look at him. This wasn't really happening to her, she thought. It was a horrible nightmare, a hideous dream from which she would awaken at any moment.

The doctor picked up a long, thick tree branch and waved it

at her. He was going to save her after all, Vanessa thought. But he only toyed with her, taunting her by holding the branch mere inches out of her reach. He was teasing her unmercifully.

"Help me, please. Let me grasp the limb," Vanessa said as her feet and ankles disappeared into the mire.

"No one can help you, Vanessa. I never thought I would succeed in getting rid of you, but at last I have. It was I who tried to push you from the cliff. It was I who shot at you in the wood. I had thought you dead, but then you came back. I couldn't let you live, Vanessa. You had to die like the others."

"Others?" She continued to struggle.

He laughed deep in his throat. "Your father tried to deny me what is mine. He was the one who was in my debt and he would not repay that debt. He tricked me. He told me he would leave the Mallory lands and properties to me if I would not tell what I knew. I killed him for that inheritance, but he tricked me. He left everything to Skull Point. But I'll get it all in time. First, I must get rid of you so you can't lay claim to what is yours."

The soggy earth crept over her ankles, up toward her knees.

"I can't let you live. You are a threat. You'll take away all that is owed to me. Simon said he will help me get what is rightfully owed to me. He knew I stole the bloodstone ring. I was going to offer it to you in exchange for the properties but he took it away from me. He promised to help me if I gave him the ring. I know I was drunk and talked too much to Simon. I should not have told him everything, but he'll keep quiet. He'll help me. He is my friend."

"Take the Mallory properties, if that is what you want so badly. I'll give them to you. Take whatever you wish. I'll trade my life for whatever you feel the Mallory family owes you."

"No, I could not face you now that you know the terrible things I've done. You must die like the others. Like your father and mother."

"But they are not dead," Vanessa sobbed. "My father and mother are alive. They are living in Bloodstone. I've seen them. I've talked with them. Whatever harm you do to me, you will still have them to reckon with."

"They're dead, I tell you. I should know. It was I who killed them. And I will kill you, Vanessa. You must die. You must die like the others."

"You're stark raving mad. You can't kill me and get away with it."

"Oh, but I can. Nobody will know your body is lying in that bog. They will think you left on the tide with the young sea captain. No one will ever suspect."

"But my parents...they'll know."

"You can't trick me as your father tricked me. They are dead. Everyone knows that they're dead."

"No. They are not dead." Vanessa felt the bog sucking her down. Her knees were covered. She was sinking deeper and deeper.

"The more you struggle the faster it will swallow you up," the doctor said. Again he waved the branch inches out of her reach. "I cannot help torturing you just a bit with this limb," he said. "It is such exquisite torture. Now you know how your father made me sweat."

"I'm sure you're wrong, Doctor. Father would never torment a man for any reason. He is not that kind of person. You must have imagined it all in your twisted mind."

"Twisted," he yelled, throwing down the branch. It landed across the surface of the bog, inches away from Vanessa's hand. "It is you who are insane. Everyone knows you're crazy."

Vanessa tried to ease herself forward. She felt the bog sucking her deeper into its slimy depths. She kept her eyes on Doctor Smithers but her hand moved out and touched the end of the long, thick branch. He hadn't seen her grasp it. He was laughing up at the sky.

"Vanessa," he said, resting his gaze on her frightened face. "You will never know the satisfaction I will feel once you are gone. I will have no one else to torment me."

"Simon will torment you," Vanessa said, tightening her grip around the end of the branch. She kept her eyes fixed on his face. "Simon knows the things you've done. Do you think he will let you have the properties? Don't be a fool, Doctor. Simon will use you and bleed you until you can't stand it anymore. Then you will have to kill again, just as you killed before. There will be no end to it, Doctor Smithers. You will have to kill and kill and kill again."

He was staring at her. His eyes were like burning sparks in the night. "No. You'll be the last. It will end with you."

"It will never end." She tried to lift the branch. It was heavier than she thought. She'd only been able to grip the farthest end and the leverage was off. She reached out slowly and put both hands around the end. "You know as well as I that Simon will never let you have what you wish. He is a very ambitious old man. He wants wealth and power and will stop at nothing to get it. As long as Simon has a hold over your head he will bleed you dry. You'll fall under his yoke just as Will Wilkins and Sam Hastings did. They can't move without Simon's nod."

She found that with both hands she could wield the branch. She tried not to think of the thick, marshy bog that was creeping up around her. She kept her eyes firmly fixed on Doctor Smithers' face.

With a quick fast sweep she swung the branch and struck the doctor on his shins. He let out a howl and grabbed his legs. Again Vanessa hit him with the branch, this time on the side, throwing him off balance. He fell...face down into the marshy bog. He flailed his arms and legs, trying to right himself, trying to grasp onto something that would keep him from sinking. He was face down on the surface of the bog, and with all his struggling about it only took a few moments before he had drowned.

Vanessa couldn't keep back her terrified screams. She had not meant to topple him into the mire. She had wanted only to drive him away so that she could save herself. But it was too late to save herself, she thought. The bog was nearly up to her waist and she was sinking deeper and deeper into it.

It would be mere minutes before all was finished for her. She screamed and screamed but there was no one to hear her.

Her end was near and a strange calm suddenly came over her. She felt that she had relived all this once before. She thought about the bloodstone ring and the man from whose neck it hung suspended. She thought of the few hours of happiness she'd had with him.

Even Simon Caldwell was gone when she needed him the most. If he hadn't gone away to Devon she and Malcolm might well be married by now. The bloodstone might be restored to Bloodstone Manor and all would be righted. Justice would fall with bloodstone bright, as the poem put it.

No, she must save herself—but it was hopeless.

"Do not struggle, child," she heard a voice say. There, standing on the bank, was her old guardian. Tutrice was looking around, as if expecting to see someone else. Vanessa turned her eyes. Carl came out of the wood and stood beside Tutrice. Vanessa stared at them unbelieving, but when they picked up the long branch, Vanessa unconsciously tightened her grip around the end and they began pulling her to safety.

They worked with little effort, it seemed. Vanessa felt herself being pulled free. Her clothes were thick with mud and seemed heavier than the bog itself. They yanked and pulled and together they managed to free her from the thick, sucking mud that had tried to claim her.

When she landed on solid ground she collapsed into a dead faint. She did not feel herself being lifted up and carried away.

CHAPTER TWENTY-TWO

Vanessa awoke to the rattling of shutters and the whistling of the wind. The lamp near her bed threw an eerie light over the room, dim and shadowy. Tutrice sat dozing in a chair. When Vanessa stirred, the old woman opened her eyes. She got up and smoothed Vanessa's hair back from her face.

"Where am I?" Vanessa asked.

"Where would you be but at Bloodstone?" Tutrice said.

Vanessa tried to sit up. Tutrice eased her back onto the pillows. "Best remain in bed, child," she said. Something banged against the locked shutters. Vanessa's eyes went toward the sound. "Another storm is brewing, but we are safe here. There is no cause to worry."

"How long have I been asleep?"

"Several hours. Dawn will be breaking soon."

Dawn. The word brought back memories of a ship with blood-red sails that was supposed to carry her away. She saw Malcolm's face before her eyes. She sat bolt upright, fighting away Tutrice's restraining hands. "I must go to him. His ship sails this morning."

"No, child. It is too late for that now."

"Too late?" Vanessa's eyes widened.

"There is no need to go to him. Everything is finished."

"Has he sailed?"

Tutrice shook her head. "Not yet, lovely one. But we have no need of him anymore. All our efforts have been to no avail. The prophecy will be fulfilled someday but not by you. The bloodstone is lost, but not forever. Someday someone new will bring vengeance."

"I don't care about the bloodstone or vengeance," Vanessa said as she swung her feet over the side of the bed and got up. She pulled a wrapper around her and went toward the armoire. "I must go to him. He cannot sail without me."

"You are foolish to think you can reach him in this storm. It will be at full force soon. You must not leave Bloodstone."

"But I am going to leave Bloodstone," Vanessa said, pulling herself into some clothes. "I never want to see this place again."

Tutrice looked sad. She merely shook her head and let her shoulders slump. "There is nowhere else for you but here." She raised her eyes. "Or would you prefer to be at the bottom of the bog?"

Vanessa froze. The vivid memory of Doctor Smithers standing waving the branch flashed before her eyes. "Oh, it was horrible, Tutrice. Horrible!"

The old woman nodded. "But it is over now. He received his just reward. He was an evil and insane old man."

"But why did he want to kill me? I still don't understand."

"Doctor Smithers was mad with drink. In his mind he was all mixed up."

"But what did we have to do with him? What obligation did he feel Father owed him?"

Tutrice sighed. "I suppose I am free to tell you everything now," she said. She sat for a moment or two collecting her thoughts. "I can tell you everything now because everything is finished for us. And after I am done you will understand all the things that you've wondered about." Again she sighed.

"When we were away from Skull Point, your mother became very ill. Doctor Smithers attended her. Doctor Smithers came across certain information that I found out about only tonight. It was a well-kept secret which only your mother knew. But during her illness the doctor administered drugs. While she was only semi-conscious, Hester told her secret unknowingly. Later, the doctor confronted your father with what he knew. If your father paid for his silence, the doctor said, the secret would go no further."

"What secret?"

Tutrice held up her hand. "Your father paid handsomely for Doctor Smithers' silence. Then your parents heard of your supposed drowning. Thinking you dead, your father refused to pay any more. He and Doctor Smithers had a violent quarrel. Doctor Smithers pushed your father down the stairs and was under the impression that he had killed him.

"The doctor would not return to the house. He thought he had left your mother to die. He went mad and took to drink to soothe his madness. His one obsession was drink and he drowned himself in it. He had convinced himself that the Mallory properties belonged to him. That is what your father and he had argued about the night he pushed your father down the stairs.

"When you returned he looked upon you as a threat. You made no secret of the fact that you found your father and mother alive and living here. The doctor thought you were trying to trick him into confessing his supposed crimes and do him out of the claim he believed he had on your properties. Out of panic he felt he had to kill you to keep you still."

"But tell me. What secret was Father so afraid of having known?"

Tutrice looked at her for a long moment. She sighed. Holding her eyes fixed firmly on Vanessa's innocent face she said, "You are not a Mallory, Vanessa. Jeremiah Mallory is not your father."

Vanessa felt her knees go weak. She dropped the cloak she had picked up. "Not a Mallory?" Her jaw dropped, her eyes widened.

Tutrice shook her head. "I never knew. As long as I have lived in this house, which was long before you were born, I never suspected. Your mother kept her secret well. Even with all my magic, it was never revealed to me that you were not a Mallory child, not until Hester admitted it to us tonight. Even the powers of darkness did not enlighten me as to Hester's secret."

Vanessa just stood there, too taken aback to speak. She

merely stared at the old woman.

"When you told us that you could not touch the bloodstone I began to suspect. We held a voodoo mass at the altar of skulls."

Vanessa nodded in spite of herself. She could see it all vividly, that pile of human bones, the grotesque atmosphere, the billowing smoke, the writhing, twisting, moaning naked figures on the floor of the cavern. She shivered in disgust but said nothing.

"The fire told me nothing. It merely said that you were responsible. We construed that to mean that you were responsible for bringing the bloodstone here. Even Carl thought that is what the voice meant. But still I was not convinced. They threatened to take away my powers if I did not insist upon your bringing the stone back. It was your mother who finally told me her secret."

"What...what did Mother say?" Vanessa stammered.

"She told me you were not a Mallory child. She thought she would never have to tell anyone that. Jeremiah knew, of course. So did Doctor Smithers." Again Tutrice paused. She started to move aimlessly about the room. "I can tell you everything now because I know you are not the last Mallory. Jeremiah holds that distinction. But alas, it is too late for him to help me."

"Help you?"

Tutrice nodded. "Do you remember the fairy story I told you, the one you enjoyed hearing so often?"

Vanessa nodded her head.

"Many, many years ago your great-great-grandfather killed the man who built this house. Mallory men never built Bloodstone. It was constructed by a man named Justice." She straightened up as far as her old, crooked body would permit. "My name is Justice. Tutrice Justice. Bloodstone belongs to me."

The wind rushed against the house, giving impetus to her words.

"You?" Vanessa gasped.

"Yes. This house belongs to me. I am the 'Justice' in the Bible." She looked heavenward. "Justice will fall with bloodstone bright," she said. Her eyes lowered and fixed themselves on Vanessa. "From generation to generation my family has sworn vengeance against the Mallorys. Each generation failed in their purpose. I could never understand my unnatural affection for you, but of course I understand it now that I know you were not of Mallory blood. I was raised to hate all Mallorys, yet I loved you and I came to love your parents. I dishonored my own people because of that affection. Vengeance can never fall on this house...or on the murderer of my ancestor. It is all too late for that now. It must wait for another time."

Vanessa stood there staring at the old woman. When Tutrice stopped speaking Vanessa stammered until she found her voice. "But who am I?" she managed to ask. "If Jeremiah is not my father, then who is?"

"Simon Caldwell."

Vanessa felt herself go weak all over. She gripped the back of a chair for support. "Simon Caldwell?" she gasped. "I can't believe it."

"That is the name your mother provided me with. She and Simon were lovers before she married Jeremiah. After the marriage she continued to see Simon. When she bore you, no one, not even Simon Caldwell himself, knew that you were not Jeremiah's child."

"Simon Caldwell." Vanessa sank down into the chair. She folded her hands in her lap and stared down at the floor. She shook her head. "I don't believe it. It isn't true." She looked up at Tutrice. "I'm a Mallory, I tell you."

Tutrice moved her head from side to side. "You are not a Mallory. The fact that you could not touch the bloodstone proves that. In the story, if you will remember, the stone was taken by a sea captain. The daughter was the only one who could bring it back through her love both for the captain and for her father. The story is not entirely fictitious. I told you what happened to the bloodstone, but I did not tell you that the sea captain was one of Jeremiah's ancestors. And I did not tell you that he killed the girl's father and stole both the stone and the young maiden. The true story did not have a happy ending. The captain abandoned the girl. He left her, taking the bloodstone with him. It was prophesied that the only one who could return the bloodstone ring was the last surviving member of the murderer's family. And the girl who was abandoned...I am a descendant of that girl."

Tutrice came to her and touched her trembling shoulders. "There is nothing to cry about. We have both found out too late. If I had but known long ago, things would have been much different. I would have been able to do what had to be done when we were in Casco Bay."

Vanessa raised her head. "Casco Bay?" she asked, still sobbing. She searched for a handkerchief and wiped her eyes.

"Ah, but enough of that for now," Tutrice said, slapping her hands on her thighs. "I've said enough. It is all over and there is nothing we can do about it. All this has been for nothing."

"Why haven't you told me all this before? I mean about the story, about the murder of your great-great-grandfather?"

"I believed you to be a Mallory. Vengeance could be reaped only through the last survivor of the Mallory family. I knew that if I told you the truth I would not receive your help. You had to do it on your own. No one could help you."

"But my father...Jeremiah. He must bring the bloodstone back."

Tutrice nodded gravely. "Yes, your father is the only one who would have been able to bring justice to fall. But he will never leave Bloodstone...so all is lost for now."

Vanessa looked around the room. "It doesn't seem possible. All this is yours," she said, admiring the handsome appointments of the room. "This house was never mine. You are its mistress."

"I never really wanted it for myself," Tutrice said. "You were the only family I had and when the bloodstone was returned, I intended to give Bloodstone to you."

"Oh, Tutrice," Vanessa cried, throwing herself into the old woman's arms. "I've treated you so shabbily all these years, and you were so good."

"There, there, child. You never treated me shabbily. You have always loved me, I know that." She kissed Vanessa's brow. "We will always be together. Nothing can separate us. We will stay at Bloodstone until the stone is returned. Then the house will fall and the prophecy will be fulfilled."

"Simon has the stone. He will give it to me. I'll get it for you, Tutrice."

"You will not be able to touch the stone," Tutrice told her. "It will burn your hand. There is an evil in the stone, a strange evil. Jeremiah is the only man who will be able to return the stone to this house."

"Then we will make him return it. We will make him go to Simon and bring the stone back."

"Jeremiah can never leave this house...not now."

"Why? Why can't he leave?"

"Don't you know?"

Vanessa shook her head.

"But surely you suspect."

Hester tapped on the door. Jeremiah was standing behind her. "I see you are rested," Hester said as she came into the room. Her eyes traveled to Tutrice. The old woman nodded.

"Tutrice has told you then?" She sighed and tears began to fill her eyes. "I am sorry, Vanessa. I know I should have told you a long time ago, but I just could not bring myself to hurt Jeremiah. He has always been good to me."

Jeremiah came to her and put his arm around his wife's waist. "I've always loved you, Hester," he said. "After Doctor Smithers told me I thought I would hate you, but I could not bring myself to hate you. We are together. We have each other. Nothing else matters."

"The bloodstone matters," Vanessa said sharply. "You must put everything right for Tutrice, Father. You must go to Simon Caldwell and bring the stone here. Tutrice must not go without what is rightfully hers."

"But I cannot go," Jeremiah said. "Surely you know why?"

"I don't know why."

Jeremiah, Hester, and Tutrice exchanged looks. Tutrice shrugged her shoulders and turned away.

Vanessa looked from one to the other. She would have to take matters into her own hands. "If you will not go, then I must go," she said, snatching up her cape and hood.

"You can do nothing," Tutrice said.

"I can try," Vanessa answered.

"But the storm," Hester said.

"I'll manage," Vanessa said as she swept the cloak around her and pulled the hood over her head. "I will manage," she repeated as she brushed past them and ran down the stairs and out into the howling gale.

No one tried to stop her.

CHAPTER TWENTY-THREE

She fought her way to the coach house and stable, saddled her horse and mounted it. The horse reared and whinnied as she spurred it out into the driving rain. Lightning cracked and split the big tree just outside the stables. One huge limb came down clear across the drive directly behind Vanessa. Another great arm of the tree smashed down through the coach-house roof. The horse reared again, but Vanessa held tight to the reins and brought him under control.

The night was black and wild. Vanessa galloped through the wind and the storm, not caring about the dangers that surrounded her. She felt driven, but by a different force. It was out of love that she searched now for the bloodstone...out of love for a lonely old woman who had spent a lifetime trying to make her happy.

She would go to Simon's house—her father's house. She would carry the bloodstone back somehow. She would repay Tutrice's kindness. Then she would fly to Malcolm and sail away with him, to wherever he wanted to take her.

The houses were all shuttered tight. She could imagine the people all huddled inside, waiting out the fury of the gale. She felt her clothes streaming behind her as she galloped through the town and turned into the drive of Simon's house. She tethered the horse under the shelter of the portico and banged on the door. She had to bang several times before the door was cracked open.

When Simon saw her standing there he pulled the door open

quickly and hurried her inside. The wind sent the crystals in the huge chandelier dancing.

"Vanessa. Good Lord, child. What are you doing out in this storm?"

"I've come for the bloodstone, Simon. Give it to me."

"Are you out of your head, girl? This is hardly any kind of weather to be riding about in for the sake of a ring."

"Please, Simon. I have no time to explain or to argue. Give me the ring and let me be on my way. I've kept my part of the bargain we made. I've gotten the townspeople to oppose the factory. Now give me the ring."

"But I don't have it," Simon said. "I've returned it to its rightful owner."

Vanessa narrowed her eyes. "I don't believe you," she said, brushing past him and going into the study. She went over to the cabinet that stood against the wall and pulled open the top drawer. It was empty. She whirled on Simon. "Where is it?" she demanded.

"I told you, child. I returned it to Malcolm. There was something very strange about that stone. I felt it was haunting me. I didn't want it in the house. He has it aboard the *Sea Serpent*."

As she studied his face she could see the resemblance. Yes, he was her father. She'd never noticed that they had the same color eyes, the same solid chin, the same sweeping brow. His hair was sparse and gray, but Vanessa knew that it had been the color of her own at one time.

This man was her father. It was almost impossible to believe, but it must be true. She wondered if Simon himself knew the truth. But he was looking at her in his usual cold way and she decided that he did not know her true identity.

And he would never know, she decided as she stood there facing him. She would only make the truth known if she learned that Simon tried to do the people of Skull Point out of their rights to the Mallory properties. She'd bring the roof down around his head if he pulled any trickery.

"Vanessa, is that you?" Brian called as he came in from

another part of the house. "Good heavens, Vanessa, you must be mad to be out in this storm."

"I'm mad, all right," she said. Brian came to her but she restrained him by putting up a defensive hand. "Please, Brian, I would appreciate it if you did not touch me. You've caused enough trouble as it is." She glanced at Simon, then back to Brian. "Do you know about the bloodstone ring?"

"Yes," Brian said. "Simon gave it back to that sailor."

"Captain Drew?"

Brian nodded. He hated the man so much he refused to utter his name. He wouldn't permit himself to think that the man *had* a name.

"The ship is still at anchor in the bay?" she asked.

"Of course. They'd be fools to try to weather this storm."

Vanessa whirled on him. "Everyone is a fool when they believe strongly in something," she said. "One must be somewhat of a fool if one is to be happy in life. It is you staid and sensible ones who merely exist. You don't live, you exist. Call me mad, call me a fool, call me anything you wish, but remember this—I am a woman who has lived life fully. I have had more than just a day-to-day existence. I have found true love and I would rather die than not have found it. If it takes madness to find true love and happiness, then thank God I'm mad. If it takes a fool to fall in love, then thank God I'm a fool."

She swept past Simon and Brian and went back out into the storm, slamming the door solidly behind her. That part of her life was finished, she thought as she again mounted her horse. She was going to Malcolm. He had the bloodstone. If it took every ounce of strength in her body she would bring the bloodstone back to Tutrice. She'd beg Malcolm to carry it there. He'd listen to her story. He would understand. He loved her. He would want to make her happy. And then they would sail away to wherever the winds took them.

The rain lashed at her, drenching her to the skin. But she did not care about the rain or the wind or the storm. The horse kept his head straight into the wind and carried Vanessa back through the town and down toward the wind-tossed harbor.

The *Sea Serpent* pitched and swayed on the rough waters. Her sails were still secured. Vanessa dismounted near a storage shed and hurried the horse inside. She hitched it firmly and went back out into the rain. She ran to the edge of the wharf and peered out at the huge black-and-red ship that would carry Malcolm away from her. She had to reach him. It was useless to shout to Malcolm; her voice would be lost on the wind.

She searched for some means of transportation out to the large ship. Below her was a rock landing with steps leading down to where a small rowboat was tied. It looked too flimsy to weather the stormy sea but she had to try.

She ran to the landing and climbed into the dinghy. The boat rocked dangerously as she untied the line. It pitched and rolled as she fought with the oars, maneuvering the tiny boat out into the lashing, bobbing sea. The spray hit her face. The wind ripped the hood from her head. Her hair flew out, like trailing tentacles. She rowed, feeling the ache in her arms, the strain in her shoulders. She pulled with all her might, inching the boat closer and closer to Malcolm's ship.

There was nothing about her but churning, crashing water. The boat was low in the water, the bottom filling with sea water. Vanessa's feet were cold, her hands numb, her back pained as she tugged at the oars, dragging them through the thrashing waves, fighting the wind, battling the rain.

For what seemed an eternity she fought to keep the tiny boat afloat and on course. At last the boat banged dully against the side of the huge ship. Her little boat was lower in the water as she pushed herself along the hull, searching for a ladder. She cupped her hands around her mouth and yelled out. The wind seemed to drown her words.

Then a miracle happened. Someone on deck looked over the side and saw her far below. She saw the man scurry away and reappear moments later. He threw down a rope ladder. She stepped onto it just as the tiny boat dipped under a wave and began to sink.

Malcolm pulled her into his arms the moment she was over the rail. "Oh, you foolish, wonderful darling," he gushed as he kissed her eyes, her hair, her mouth.

"I could not let you leave, Malcolm. I had to explain."

"There is nothing to explain. I should have known you would come to me. I was insane to think you could love a man like that. Oh, Vanessa, I wanted so badly to go to you, to bring you here. But my time ashore was over and I was not permitted to return."

She frowned up into his face. "I don't understand," she said.

"You will, my darling...you will. But come. You must get into dry clothes." He took her hand and pulled her toward the shelter of his cabin.

Once the door closed, they found themselves locked in a passionate embrace. The world was theirs. Time was theirs. They were in an eternity of their own and nothing could ever separate them again.

When their embrace ended Vanessa looked into Malcolm's face and smiled. "Oh, Malcolm, I do love you. I love you more than my own life."

"What is life without you, my beloved?" he said. "This is all the life I want...and I am holding it in my arms."

Again they kissed.

Vanessa stiffened suddenly. "I must have the bloodstone," she said, easing herself away from him. "Simon said he gave it to you."

"The bloodstone!" Malcolm's face darkened. "You came for the bloodstone?"

Vanessa touched her lips to his. "Not only for the bloodstone, Malcolm. I came for you, of course. But I must return the bloodstone to Tutrice. The prophecy will then be fulfilled and I will be able to leave with you whenever you say."

"But we sail in a few hours."

"I will be back in a few hours."

"That isn't possible. You can't leave again. I won't let you leave. You came back for me, not for this accursed stone," he said. He ripped the stone and its cord from around his neck and threw them across the cabin.

Vanessa ran to where the stone lay and picked it up. It felt warm to the touch, but she tightened her fist around it.

"Leave it," Malcolm shouted.

"No, you don't understand, my darling. Let me explain." She hurriedly told him all that Tutrice had told her. She told him her mother's secret and of the fairy story. When she finished she found herself breathless.

"Then what concern is it to you? You are Simon's child. You are not a Mallory. Why do you feel responsible for returning the bloodstone?"

"I owe it to Tutrice. She was duped all these years. She lived her life for me. This is my chance to repay her for everything she's done. I must return it, Malcolm. Can't you see that?"

The bloodstone was beginning to burn her palm. The fire inside the stone was getting more intense as the seconds passed.

"Trust me, darling. Believe in me," Vanessa begged. The stone was growing so hot she could not hold it. She winced with pain and dropped it to the floor. They stood there staring down at it. "Help me, Malcolm...please help me," she implored.

He looked into her face, then back down to where the stone lay. He stooped over and picked it up. "I cannot. It is impossible for me to return to the land."

"Why? Why are you so bent on not going back?"

"I cannot go back. It is a bargain I made many years ago. The pact can never be broken. I must stay aboard this ship. You must also now that you have come aboard because of your love for me."

"But no pact was ever made that couldn't be broken. You must return with me, just for a short while."

He stared down into the fiery depths of the stone. "No. I cannot," he said sadly. "And neither can you," he added, raising his eyes to hers.

She snatched the stone from his hand. Before Malcolm could stop her she rushed out onto the deck, slipping the cord about her neck as she ran.

"No, Vanessa," he yelled. "Don't leave. You don't know what you're doing."

She did not hear his words. She ran across the deck toward the rail and paused there looking down. There was no escape.

"No, Vanessa," Malcolm shouted. "No. Please...."

Vanessa threw herself over the side and fell down, down, down, into the churning, swirling water. She felt the heat of the stone around her neck. It suddenly seemed heavier. It was pulling her under the waves.

She splashed and kicked and flailed her arms, but the stone was weighing her under. She was sinking, sinking beneath the water, toward the floor of the sea.

She was only slightly conscious of arms about her. It took several seconds before she felt the strength of him, buoying her up. His hands slipped the stone from around her neck and at once she felt lighter...freer. She rose...rose up to breathe air. She gulped in great quantities of it as her head broke the surface. Malcolm's face was next to hers. She wrapped her arms around him.

"Don't struggle," he managed to say as the waves crashed over them. "Try to move your arms and legs. Hang on to me."

She clung to him as he started to swim back toward the rope ladder that hung over the side of the *Sea Serpent.*

"No," Vanessa cried. She fought him off and, seeing the bloodstone glimmer, she again snatched it from his hand

Almost immediately the stone pulled her under. Malcolm embraced her and they sank deeper and deeper, locked in each other's arms.

CHAPTER TWENTY-FOUR

Simon Caldwell and Brian McGrath stood in the center of the crowd of people who were positioned in the center of the street, listening to the approaching clamor.

"They're coming," Simon called as the townspeople all rallied behind him, ready to defend the town against the oncoming monsters who were intent upon digging a foundation for a new factory.

They didn't expect the awesomeness of those monsters, however. "What are they?" Brian asked, his eyes wide. Huge yellow bulldozers and chugging steam shovels appeared in the distance. Giant lumbering trucks, all painted in brilliant colors, massive heavy-duty equipment, all belching smoke and running without aid of horse or mule, huffed and puffed into town. The very ground beneath their feet shook as the motor vehicles moved slowly on Skull Point. They came straight at the gathered throng. Closer and closer and closer.

"Stop! Stop!" Simon yelled, but the trucks and equipment lumbered directly down upon them.

"Am I crazy?" Jenny Hastings yelled as the wheels of the motor trucks dug deep ridges into the dirt road. "What is happening? I've never seen anything like it."

"They're some kind of monsters," Will Wilkins said. "I can't believe my eyes."

They all stared in disbelief at the horde of vehicles that descended upon them.

The trucks and heavy duty equipment stopped dead center

of town. Two men dressed in odd clothes—heavy boots, tight work pants, little metal hats on their heads—began to converse. Simon hurried over to them.

"Please," he said. "You must send these things away."

"Boy, some dump, huh?" one of the men said to the other.

Simon put his hand on the man's arm. "You must listen to us," he said.

"Look at that old relic up there on the bluff," the other man said. "That place must be a couple of hundred years old."

"It's falling apart," the first man said. "We were looking around inside that trap just last week. Nothing in that old barn but a lot of spiders and cobwebs and bats. The place is really in awful shape. It won't take more than the bulldozer to pull it down."

"You don't think we'll need the crane and ball?"

"Nah."

"Please," Simon pleaded. "I must insist"—tugging at the man's sleeve. "The governor is going to issue a stop order for this project of yours," he yelled.

"The whole town is falling to pieces. One quick trip with the bulldozer should level it to rubble."

"Where's the plant going to be?"

Simon was in a rage. They were ignoring him completely. All the townspeople started to shout and shake their fists, but it was as if they weren't there. Simon sputtered and yelled and shook his arms but the men seemed to be looking right through him.

"Up on the bluff where that old red-and-black monster is sitting now."

"I wonder why anybody would want to live in a monstrosity like that. Ugh, it gives me the willies just looking at it."

"It's supposed to give you the willies, Mack. This here place used to be called Skull Point. It had to do with pirates or something away back a long time, before the Civil War. There was a hurricane and the whole blooming town was swept out to sea. Not one single body was ever recovered. But some folks said they saw lights on in some of the ruins after the storm. The town folk were supposed to have come up out of the sea and reclaimed their homes. The place is haunted, according to some."

They both laughed and motioned for the modern-day equipment to move on Bloodstone.

* * * * * *

Malcolm heard the racket and knocked away one of the boards that covered the window. He stared out at the equipment that was coming closer to the house.

"What is it?" Vanessa asked as the bulldozer groaned and roared and moved nearer and nearer to the old mansion.

"I don't know," Malcolm said. "I've never seen anything like it before. They are some kind of metal monster."

The two of them stood beneath the splendor of the ornate chandelier. The sitting room was impeccably clean and sparkling. The crystals over their head tinkled softly in the atmosphere of the lovely yellow-and-cream room. The mahogany tables gleamed from recent waxing. The tiny china cups rattled daintily in their cabinets as the vehicles pounded the ground outside and shook the house's foundation.

"I don't understand it," Vanessa said. She gripped Malcolm's arm. He wrapped his arm around her waist and pulled her close.

"Have no fear, children," Tutrice said as she came to stand behind them. Jeremiah and Hester appeared in the doorway. "You have nothing to be afraid of. Nothing can destroy Bloodstone now," she said, nodding to the brilliant red-and-black stone that sat on the mantle. "Bloodstone will always be here for those who find love."

"But they'll kill us."

Tutrice smiled. "No," she said through her sad smile. She sighed. "They will never kill you, my darlings. You will live forever. One cannot kill love." Again she sighed. "I was wrong to want to give you life...the young and foolish life to which I thought you were entitled. But I learned that one cannot give something one does not possess. We were always gone from this world, my child. Don't you know that now? Ever since that first time many years ago when you cast yourself into the sea at Casco Bay your fate was sealed. You only live now in love."

The huge lumbering machines moved in on the crumbling mansion. Their blunt thick teeth chewed out the blood red stones. The walls creaked, the roof sagged. The house seemed to come apart at the seams.

Malcolm walked out of the room, taking Vanessa with him. They walked down the overgrown lawn to the edge of the bluff and looked out at the sea. Their arms went around each other and they saw a ship with blood-red sails appear on the horizon. The sun was making it glow like a jewel on the water.

"Tomorrow," Malcolm said, pulling Vanessa tight against him. "Tomorrow, my darling."

"Yes, tomorrow," she replied as he took her in his arms and kissed her passionately. Then they turned and went slowly back toward Bloodstone, where Tutrice stood in the door waiting for them.

It was a glorious day. They began to run, hand in hand.

ABOUT THE AUTHOR

VICTOR J. BANIS is the critically acclaimed author ("...a master storyteller"—*Publishers Weekly*) of more than 200 published novels and numerous shorter works in a career spanning nearly a half century. A longtime Californian, he lives and writes now in West Virginia's beautiful Blue Ridge region.

www.ingramcontent.com/pod-product-compliance
Lightning Source LLC
Chambersburg PA
CBHW050737250626
47155CB00005B/1812